bagels and betrayal

Snow Falls Alaska Cozy - 3

wendy meadows

Majestic Owl Publishing LLC
P.O. Box 997
Newport, NH 03773

 Created with Vellum

chapter one

It felt strange being in North Carolina. Yes, strange. Bethany Lights should have felt right at home, but she didn't. Even though she had only been living in Snow Falls, Alaska for a short time, somehow that short period had allowed the rest of the world to transform into a strange creature that her heart could barely recognize.

Snow Falls, Alaska was a different world that changed a person in a way that Bethany struggled to understand. Bethany felt as though she had somehow always belonged in Snow Falls, but had missed the boat and was just now swimming ashore. Was she ready to leave her new home so quickly and return to a place that seemed to scorn her very presence? Bethany wasn't sure.

"Maybe this wasn't such a good idea," she whispered as her eyes studied a lovely two-story Victorian home perched comfortably in front of a large, sleepy lake glimmering in the late autumn sun.

"Here's your luggage, miss," a grumpy cab driver spoke up.

Bethany turned her head, spotting a depressed-looking man wearing an old baseball cap and standing next to a run-down yellow cab.

"Oh, thank you. Mr. Gray, I...one minute." Bethany quickly snapped open a green purse and searched for some money. A powerful gust of cold autumn wind blasted by, throwing her silky red hair into a dance filled with lazy multi-colored leaves. "I'll find you a tip."

Davy Gray set two black suitcases down onto a gravel driveway that felt deserted. He was a man who had recently suffered through a hideous divorce. Davy's ex-wife, a woman who'd decided that a sleazy lawyer could somehow replace a twenty-year marriage without causing harm or damage, had taken him to the bank and stolen a great sum of money, not to mention a nice house, twenty-four acres of land, a new truck, a boat...everything. Teaming up with a sleazy lawyer had certainly paid off for her. They'd left Davy with only a few pennies and a run-down truck on its last leg. His brother, who owned a cab business, had tossed Davy a bone and given him a job with the company—for the time being, at least. No one knew what Davy's plans were and where the poor guy would end up...not even Davy.

"There's no need—"

"Oh, I always leave a good tip. It's the proper thing to do," Bethany insisted.

Davy examined the beautiful woman, who reminded him of an actress he couldn't quite remember. Davy was sure the actress his mind was trying to find didn't have red hair like Bethany, though the woman fishing through a fussy purse carried an uncanny resemblance to her. No matter. Davy wasn't really in the mood to play "name that face." He was hungry and it was getting close to supper time. Maybe he would go eat at the local Chick-Fil-A or get some Captain D's? His brother's wife wasn't exactly the greatest cook in the world—or the nicest person.

"Well, thank you."

Bethany found a twenty-dollar bill. "Here you go," she told Davy, offering a kind smile.

Davy accepted the money with a reluctant hand. He guessed all Bethany saw was a beaten-down man wearing an old gray coat and a pair of worn-down tan slacks—not much of a man.

"Thank you. Uh, want me to carry your luggage to the front porch?"

Before Bethany could answer, another powerful blast of cold wind struck her. The wind grabbed the blue hat Bethany was wearing with fast hands. She tucked her head down and waited for the wind to pass. "I forgot how cold it could be up here on the lake."

"Supposed to snow tonight." Davy lifted his eyes and studied a low, gray sky slowly growing pregnant with a snowstorm. Icy wind whispered under the sky, dancing through rustling trees, shedding beautiful autumn leaves, and then skipping across the surface of a large lake, which reflected the sky and dancing leaves in its eyes. Miles of lonely woods surrounded the lake. The Victorian house sat up on top of Old Wolf Mountain all alone on private land. How much private land? Supposedly, the Lights owned close to five thousand acres of lush mountain land on top of Old Wolf Mountain, though Davy believed the count was closer to seven thousand. The Lights family was a very wealthy family, that much was for sure—at least in Davy's eyes. He didn't think a simple twenty-dollar tip would damage Bethany's money purse badly.

"Yes, that's what I heard." Bethany glanced around. She didn't see any vehicles parked in the main driveway. *No one is here. Mother was very kind to let me come stay at the mountain home and rest. Well, at least that's what I told mother. The truth is, Julie is in danger, and I needed to get her away from Snow Falls. I couldn't tell mother that because she would have called in the army.*

"Julie, are you ready?"

Julie Walsh drew in an uneasy breath, and then pulled

herself out of the back of Davy's cab like a broken rag doll trying to find her legs.

"I didn't realize we were up so far…alone. I almost feel like I'm back on Icy Mountain," she told Bethany as her eyes walked around a strange but beautiful land.

Davy looked over at Julie. Julie, like Bethany, was a very beautiful woman—a British woman who spoke with a thick British accent. He liked how Julie's black hair rested on a pair of soft shoulders that seemed to belong to a caring soul. Julie reminded him of a 1940s World War II nurse who tended to wounded soldiers and offered soothing words of hope and care.

"I'll get your luggage, miss."

"Thank you." Julie walked over to Bethany as her eyes locked onto the Victorian house. "It's lovely," she spoke in a quick voice, hugging a simple navy coat. "But I didn't realize we would be so far up…alone."

"Honey, someone called and threatened your life. I got you out of Snow Falls as fast as I could, without looking overly suspicious and brought you to the only place I felt you would be safe," Bethany whispered. She nodded toward the Victorian house. "I spent countless summers up here with my parents as a little girl and a young teenager. I know this land, and I know that house like I know the back of my hand." Bethany turned and pointed down a long gravel road. "Mr. Gray, will you lock the main gate when you leave?"

"I will," Davy promised, pulling two green suitcases out of a trunk that smelled of oil and dust. He set the suitcases down next to Julie. "It's an hour's drive back to the bottom of the mountain, and another half-hour drive back to town. You ladies are up here alone."

Davy felt that leaving two ladies alone on the top of a high mountain wasn't such a good idea. Usually, his gut didn't offer ill-advised counsel. "Uh, is there a certain time you want me to be back to pick you up?"

"We're staying for two weeks. My mother has stocked the home with food, firewood, and gas for the built-in generators." Bethany scanned the beautiful, chilly afternoon again with careful eyes. Was someone hiding in the woods? Watching...waiting to strike? *Julie and I rented a car and drove from Snow Falls all the way to Seattle before we boarded a plane. I didn't see anyone following us the entire time or spot any suspicious person on the two flights we took from Seattle to Raleigh. If anyone is hiding and watching...I just pray we're alone.* "Mr. Gray, can you be back two weeks from today?"

"Sure," Davy nodded without showing much enthusiasm. Why was it any of his business why Bethany and Julie were staying up on the top of a lonely mountain? It was no secret that the Lights family were loaded and even a bit...eccentric. Bethany Lights seemed like a normal lady, but who knew? Maybe Bethany and Julie were bona fide nuts? Davy doubted if his ill thoughts were true, but again, what was it any of his business? He hadn't seen Bethany since his teenage years. "I guess I'll be going. But before I do...uh, mind if I ask you a question?"

"I suppose," Bethany agreed.

"You don't recognize me, do you?" Davy asked.

Bethany's eyes narrowed into a curious expression. She quickly studied a man of average height and build that made her think of beardless Victor French. "Uh, no. I'm sorry I don't, Mr. Gray."

Davy nodded. He had only told Bethany and Julie his last name. "Does the name 'Sickly Davy' ring a bell?"

"Sickly Davy?" Bethany continued to stare at Davy for a few seconds, and then a lightbulb went off inside her mind. "Are you Davy Andrew Gray?" she quickly asked.

Davy nodded. "Better known as 'Sickly Davy' because I had cancer when we went to school together." Davy dropped his eyes, looked at a worn-down pair of boots he was wearing, and then shook his head. "It's alright that you don't recognize me. I missed a lot of school, and even when I was in school, I was invisible. The sick kids always get pushed to the back."

Bethany could barely believe her eyes. Was she really talking to Davy Gray? *Oh, how could I have missed it? The last name Gray should have been a dead giveaway. I guess my mind is so occupied with keeping Julie safe that I overlooked a simple fact.*

"Well, it has been some years, but I remember you, Davy. At least, now I do. I'm sorry for not remembering before."

"Why would you? We all change. I used to be as skinny as a broomstick. I've maintained a healthy weight through the years, but now my hair is peppered with gray and I'm not sixteen anymore." Davy raised his eyes and looked into a beautiful face. "I married Tracy Bates. We stayed married for twenty years. We got divorced last year...ugly divorce."

"Oh, I'm sorry, I..." Bethany wasn't sure what to say. *Who was Tracy Bates? The name doesn't ring a bell.* "Forgive me, Davy, but I don't know who Tracy Bates is."

"You wouldn't. I met my wife when I went off to North Carolina State. At the time my folks were doing well. My dad owned four grocery stores..." Davy shook his head. "Well, what does it matter? The past is the past."

Davy looked around. His gut was gnawing at him, but what could he do? Bethany and Julie were grown women. "Your mother already paid for the ride in advance. I guess I'll be seeing you in two weeks."

"I guess so." Bethany's mind struggled to remember Davy. Bits and pieces of a broken past appeared. She saw a sickly young man sitting in the back of a depressing classroom that smelled of chalk dust and pencil shavings. *I remember now. Davy was always called "Sickly Davy" by the football players. He never talked much, always seemed to keep to himself. We were assigned to do a science project together once...I think we received a passing grade. My, how time passes.* "If we need anything, I'll call. My mother told me you volunteered to bring any needed supplies up—"

"I did," Davy nodded. "Your mother hired me to be at her disposal for the next two weeks." He glanced toward Julie, who offered a polite smile. "I'm the one who installed the built-in generators and made sure they were up to par and that the phone line was still in working order. Before I drove a cab, I owned Gray Electrical. Now...well, my wife made sure she took everything."

Bethany felt her heart break for Davy. Standing before her was a man who seemed to have lost the desire and enthusiasm to embrace life. What could she do? What could she say? Julie was in danger, and Bethany needed to focus on protecting her friend.

"Mr. Gray, uh...where are you staying at the moment?"

"At my brother's. He has an apartment over his garage that he's letting me use." Davy nodded toward the run-down yellow cab he was standing close to. "I'm working for him, too. That cab belongs to him. Mostly, I drive outsiders to and from the airport. The locals in Pine Lakes have little need for a cab. My brother services Pine Lakes, Green Valley, and White Ridge. He does okay..." Davy slid his mouth to a stop. He wasn't much for talking and wasn't sure why he was blabbing his jaws to Bethany.

"Davy? Uh, my mother did inform me she hired you to help us for the next two weeks. Uh...I know this may sound abrupt and a little strange, but would it be too much to ask if you might...stay up here at the lake house with me and my friend for the next two weeks?" Bethany asked in a voice that sounded uncertain rather than clear and concise.

Julie tossed Bethany a confused look. "Love?" she asked.

"I suppose I would feel safer if someone were up here with us, Julie," Bethany struggled to offer a quick answer that would soothe Julie's worry. "Davy, there are plenty of bedrooms." *I hope Davy doesn't think I'm insane for making such a request. I created an escape plan in such haste that I'm just now catching up to my own thoughts. I wanted to get Julie out of Snow Falls and to a safe location. I really didn't have time to plan matters through the way I wanted to. And now that we're here at the lake house, I feel it would be better to have someone up here with us.*

"Well..." Davy scratched at the back of his head with a thoughtful hand. "I have nothing else to do for the next two weeks. Your mother hired me to look after you, and I doubt my brother will go under if I'm not around. I was just going to drive back down the mountain and twiddle my thumbs and wait for you to call." Davy walked his eyes around. Being at the top of Old Wolf Mountain made him feel...free. Maybe spending two weeks away from the world was what the doctor ordered? It certainly couldn't hurt to take a much needed breather. "Sure. Why not? I'll need to go get clothes and other supplies. Should be back around dark if that's all right."

"That will be fine." Bethany offered a relieved smile. "Julie and I will have dinner started by then."

Davy nodded. "Sounds good," he told Bethany, and then looked around one last time. "We're supposed to be getting some snow, so we better get settled in good. I'll be back as soon as I can."

Bethany and Julie watched Davy get into his cab, wave, and then drive away.

"Well, love, I hope you know what you're doing." Julie sighed and then picked up her luggage. "We better get inside."

Bethany looked around. *We're at the lake house, and now I have to figure out what to do. Whoever called Julie isn't going to vanish into the wind.*

chapter two

Wood battered by countless winters creaked and moaned under the brown boots Julie was wearing. The wraparound porch that decorated the Victorian lake house with dazzling beauty was old and grumpy, but that simply added charm—if charm was possible in such a dire situation.

Julie felt terrified as she approached a large green door with what appeared to be a snow owl carved in the middle of it. She spotted a line of country rocking chairs sitting off to her left and a lovely porch swing hanging off to her right. Bethany carefully unlocked the front door.

"It is lovely here. Very quiet, love," she said to Bethany.

"My great-great-grandfather bought this land," Bethany explained, struggling to make a rusted lock agree with an old key. "My family has fought to keep all this land. Years back, the county threatened to take the land by force, but my parents contacted a senator friend they knew who intervened —harshly, I might add. My family has had no trouble from the county since. Not a single—come on, lock, work!—acre of land has been bothered. Come on, lock."

"Perhaps we can take a walk to the lake once we get our luggage inside?" Julie suggested.

"The lake is exquisite—oh, come on, work!" Bethany let out a loud roar and hit the lock she was fussing at with a hard hand. "Work!"

"Love, let me try." Julie stepped forward and took the set of keys Bethany was holding with a careful hand. Bethany stepped back and waited. To her relief, Julie unlocked the front door with little trouble. "I've always had a special touch." Julie smiled.

"Remind me to call you the next time I lock my keys in my SUV." Bethany smiled back and drew in a deep breath of cold air. She turned away from the front door and allowed her eyes to soak in a beautiful, lush, crisp autumn day. "It is exquisite up on the mountain. When I was a little girl, I used to love when my parents would bring me here. There was no electricity, but my parents paid more money to have a phone line run up this far. It's just peace and quiet."

A gust of cold wind ran up onto the front porch and said hello. Julie allowed the wind to touch her face without turning away. The wind, although cold, felt refreshing.

"Bethany?"

"I know." Bethany slowly turned back around and faced Julie. "You're ready to tell me about the phone call?"

"I appreciate you haven't pressed me about the phone call," Julie told Bethany in a voice filled with deep gratitude. "I was able to convince Amanda that the phone call I received was from my ex-husband and that the trip we're on right now was a much-needed holiday."

"Let's go inside and make some coffee. We'll talk more once we get settled in." Bethany threw her eyes around. "I know Davy is a stranger, Julie, but I would feel better knowing someone else is here with us. I barely remember Davy, but what I do remember about him is that he came from a decent family. I honestly feel he's a good man."

"I didn't sense anything wrong about your friend, either," Julie agreed. "I must admit, it is a bit scary being on this mountain alone. I mean, love, we were just on Icy Mountain fighting to stay alive. Now look at us." Julie let out a hopeless smile. "We're a pair, you and me."

"We sure are." Bethany picked up her luggage. "Let's go inside."

Julie retrieved her own luggage and followed Bethany into an enormous house that reflected the authenticity of the Victorian era. Bethany's mother had gone above and beyond to ensure the interior of the house was colored with antiquated paint strokes filled with brilliance and charm.

"My goodness, it's so lovely."

Bethany stepped into a large foyer that smelled of old peppermints and cherry pipe tobacco.

"Oh my...even after all these years..." Tears nearly escaped from Bethany's eyes. *Daddy's pipe tobacco. I can still smell it. I can still smell mother's peppermint.*

"Love, are you all right?"

"I'm alright," Bethany promised her friend. "Will you close and lock the front door?"

"Of course." Julie set down the two suitcases she was holding and tended to her chore. "Well," she said, feeling safer now that the front door was locked, "maybe we should go to our rooms and put our luggage up before we have coffee, love?"

Bethany stood still and looked around. A bright overhead light was shining down on her. *The electricity is on, which means the built-in generators are working. That's a plus. When I was a little girl, all we had up here were lanterns, candles, and fireplaces to give us light and warmth. It's been so many years since I've been here, but why? Why did I let that awful man control my life and make me miss out on everything I once loved?* A deep bitterness filled with pain and remorse walked into Bethany's heart like a stone soldier. *Well, there's no sense in being angry about what can't be changed. I must focus on protecting Julie. Hopefully, Davy won't be gone too long. I wasn't keen on being up on this mountain with Julie alone. I acted in such haste, I couldn't plan everything out carefully. When Julie told me her life was in danger, I acted. Now, I will have to sit back, take a deep breath, calm down, and plan.*

"The stairs are this way."

Julie picked up her luggage and followed Bethany to a staircase that seemed to lead back into a beautiful time long forgotten. She looked off to her left and spotted a doorway leading into what she assumed was a family sitting room. A second doorway off to the right stood closed. Two hallways, both settled on each side of the staircase, wandered off in two directions. Glossy wooden floors, deep-colored carpets, and old walls imbued the interior with a heartbeat that simply took Julie's breath away.

"Well, if I'm going to die, I would rather die here than at that horrible ski lodge we were trapped at."

"You're not going to die." Bethany glanced into Julie's eyes. *She's terrified. Whoever called Julie has caused my friend to become a scared, wounded animal. I don't like that.* "Come on, honey. I'll walk you upstairs."

"Sure, love." Julie followed Bethany up an antique staircase with a long green carpet running down the middle of it. She smelled dust, cherry pipe tobacco, and peppermint with each step she climbed. The steps creaked and moaned under her feet, creating a somewhat scary atmosphere. "Well, if we're not alone, then whoever might be hiding in this house knows we're here."

Bethany had to admit that the silence buzzing in her ears was troublesome. She resisted the urge to stop and look down the staircase to see whether a deadly stranger had somehow appeared at the bottom. Instead, she drew in a deep breath and continued upward. *I'm certain no one could have followed us. I'm certain that Julie and I are safe. Stay calm and stay productive.*

"Almost to the top..." Bethany said.

Julie glanced over her shoulder. No one was standing at the bottom of the staircase. She nodded and followed Bethany onto a silent landing. A single hallway ran from one side of the house to the other. Two hallways branched off the single hallway and dived north, deeper into the womb of the house. One hallway, Bethany quickly explained, was lined with bedrooms, and the second hallway led to an enormous library, a den, a music room, and a sewing room.

"This is an amazing house."

"Years and years' worth of building and work," Bethany spoke in a tired voice. "Follow me, honey."

Bethany broke off the main hallway and made her way down another shadowy hallway that stood off to her right. She carefully walked Julie down the hallway and stopped.

"The doors on the right and on the left lead into the two master bedrooms. You can take the bedroom to the left, and I'll take the bedroom to the right. When Davy returns, he can choose a room from one of two remaining bedrooms."

Julie glanced at a solid wooden door and nodded. "Meet you downstairs in the kitchen in about twenty minutes."

"Sounds good." Bethany waited until Julie entered her room, and then braced herself to enter a room she hadn't been in since...well, it felt like ages had passed. "It's been so long," Bethany spoke but stopped dead in her tracks when the bedroom door swung open.

"Oh my," she gasped out the words like blood squirting from a wound, but inside her mind, she screamed out the words.

Someone had placed a rocking chair right in front of the door. A body was sitting in the rocking chair slumped over, and the rocking chair was moving...a pair of dead arms swinging back and forth in the air. Before Bethany could react, she heard what sounded like the front door opening and closing downstairs.

*Stay calm...don't panic...don't panic...stay calm...*Panic and fear screamed into Bethany's heart so loud that the woman could barely hear her own thoughts. *Get to Julie…*

Bethany forced her legs to move. She backed out of the bedroom she had stepped into and burst into the bedroom Julie had entered. Julie was just setting her luggage down onto a large bed that required steps to reach a decent night's sleep, a bed with an old-fashioned green curtain that wrapped around it.

Julie quickly turned around to face Bethany. One look at her friend's face spoke volumes.

"Bethany—"

"There's a dead man in my bedroom. I thought I heard someone open and close the front door downstairs." Bethany searched a large bedroom filled with priceless furnishings. *Where is the telephone? There it is, on the telephone stand beside the window.* She charged across the room on hurried legs. She snatched up an old-fashioned brown telephone and dialed 911—at least, she tried.

"What is it, love...don't tell me—"

"Dead," Bethany dropped her shoulders. "The phone line must be cut."

Julie wasn't certain what to say or do. "Are you sure there's a dead man...well, of course you are. You wouldn't say such a horrible thing if it wasn't so." Words couldn't express the fear that growled in Julie's ears. "What do we do?"

Bethany put down the phone receiver she was holding with a shaking hand."

"Let's go back to my room."

"Why?"

"To make sure the man I saw is truly dead." Bethany quickly hurried to Julie, took her friend's hand, and cautiously eased back into a silent hallway. She stuck her ears down the hallway and listened for a few seconds. The coast seemed clear. "Come on..."

Julie made her way into Bethany's room and froze. A man

was sitting in a creaking rocking chair. He was lurched over with his arms swinging in the air, his fingers about two inches from the floor.

"Oh my."

Bethany let go of Julie's hand, drew in a scared breath, and forced herself to walk forward. Julie watched as the nervous woman picked up the dead man's right arm as if she were picking up a poisonous rattlesnake. Bethany checked for a pulse and found only death. She released the arm.

"He's dead, but his body is still warm. This man hasn't been dead for long."

"Do you know who the man is?" Julie asked, keeping her voice down to a mere whisper.

Bethany shook her head. She moved behind the rocking chair and examined the victim's back. "I see a gunshot wound, in the middle of the shoulder blades." *I'm looking at a man wearing a brown suit...looks to be in his twenties...his fingernails were immaculate and well taken care of. He's wearing fancy loafers...I doubt the brown suit I'm looking at was cheap.* She forced her mind to soak in every detail that her eyes could pinpoint.

"What do we do, love?" Julie's voice caused Bethany to look away from the back of the dead man.

"I'm not sure," Bethany confessed. *Davy left. I saw him drive away. There's no way he could have driven away and circled back to the house to kill the man I'm looking at. No, someone was in the house. But how? How did anyone know I was bringing Julie to Old Wolf Mountain? It makes no sense. I'm certain no one was following us when we drove from Snow Falls to Seattle. I used my personal cell phone to make every call. When I saw mother off at the Anchorage airport, I made sure I wasn't followed, and Julie stayed with Amanda and Sarah.*

Bethany struggled to expose any hidden thought that might shine a practical light on a deadly situation. "Julie, I think it's time you tell me who called you."

"I think so, too." Julie forced a pair of scared eyes away from the dead body. "The person who called me...I can't be sure, Bethany..." Julie's British accent became very heavy and very shaky. "I believe the person who called me was a man I once dated years ago before I met my ex-husband. I...ruined his career. He vowed revenge. I never made another enemy."

Before Bethany could answer, she heard the front door open.

"Someone is in the house!"

Bethany ran forward and slammed the bedroom door closed, then activated a heavy deadlock.

"Julie." Refusing to die without putting up a fight, Bethany bolted over to a cobblestone fireplace and snatched up an old fire iron. "If we're going to die, we will die fighting!"

chapter three

"Ms. Lights! Ms. Walsh!"

Davy's voice boomed up onto the second floor of the Victorian house like a wild rider yelling for a lost princess. "Ms. Lights! Ms. Walsh!"

"Davy?" Bethany lowered the fire iron she was gripping with two nervous hands.

"Bethany...could he be the killer?" Julie whispered, feeling too afraid to move. Being close to a dead body affected people on different levels. Not that Julie feared dead bodies. It was just, well, she always feared that if she got close enough to a dead body, the body might come back to life and grab her.

"I don't see how, unless there's two killers," Bethany whispered. "I don't see how Davy could have killed anyone, placed the body in this room, and escaped between the time we saw him drive off and the time I found the body." *Could there be two killers? Could Davy be a dangerous man? No. I don't see how. Besides, I went to school with Davy.*

"Ms. Lights! Ms. Walsh! Where are you? My cab...someone shot out the two front tires on my cab...Ms. Lights!. Ms. Walsh!" Davy's voice sounded urgent and breathless, as if he had run at full speed back to the house. Davy had, in fact, run back to the house as fast as he could. Being a man in his forties meant he wasn't as agile as a sixteen-year-old. Running fifty yards was enough to make Davy gasp for air.

"Wait here, Julie!" Bethany ran to the bedroom door, disengaged the lock, and prepared herself to either help an old friend or be killed by a brilliant mind. "Davy, we're up here in the bedroom!" she yelled into the hallway after she yanked open the bedroom door.

Davy heard Bethany's voice yell from her location. He slammed the front door closed and activated a sturdy lock. "Stay where you are!" With those words, Davy fought his way up a long set of stairs and found Bethany standing just outside her bedroom.

"Someone shot the two front tires of my cab out." A stream of blood was running down the right side of Davy's face.

"You're bleeding."

"I was shot at just as the cab was turning a sharp curve. I ran the cab into a tree." Davy raised a quick hand and felt his forehead, locating a small gash. "My head hit the steering wheel pretty bad. Could have been worse."

If someone shot at Davy's car, that person could have already been down the mountain road. The person I heard leave the house left after Davy drove away in his cab. Davy had a good ten-minute head start, maybe fifteen. Unless the person I heard leave the house can run like the wind, it seems like there might be two killers on the scene.

"Did you see anyone, Davy?"

"Not a soul." Davy covered his bleeding forehead with his left hand. "I'm not even sure why I'm standing here. Whoever shot the tires out of my cab could have easily filled me full of holes. It was stupid of me to run the way I did, but I was afraid whoever was shooting at the cab might take a shot at me. Figured it would be better to die trying to escape than just sitting still like a dumb duck."

"Davy...I...you better see for yourself."

"See what?" Davy looked into Bethany's tense face.

"You'll see. Come on." Bethany grabbed Davy's right arm with a firm hand and pulled the man into a bedroom that had transformed into a nightmare.

Davy followed Bethany into a strange bedroom, hitting the brakes when his eyes spotted a dead man sitting in a rocking chair.

"What in the world...what is this?"

"Do you recognize that man?" Bethany asked, hoping Davy might recognize the murder victim.

Davy spotted Julie staring at him with cautious eyes. The woman looked upset and terrified. "I don't know who that guy is, no," he offered an honest answer. "I can't see his face. He's bent forward too far, but I don't recognize the hair or the suit."

"Someone shot him in the back," Bethany explained, struggling to remain calm and productive. Panic would only frustrate any attempt to find practical answers. "I didn't hear any gunshots. I did hear someone leave the house when I walked into this bedroom."

"And someone shot the tires out of my cab, which means—"

"The shooter didn't want you to leave the mountain," Bethany finished for Davy.

"Sure seems that way." Davy shook his head. "Ms. Lights—"

"Davy, call me Bethany. And that's Julie," Bethany interrupted. "I think we're past the pleasantries here."

"Are you sure you don't recognize the victim?" Julie asked Davy pleadingly.

Davy shook his head. "I owned my own business in Pine Lakes for close to twenty years and serviced the surrounding towns. During that time, I got to know countless customers. Most customers became friends." Davy checked his left hand.

The palm was soaked with blood. "Can you get me a towel or something?"

"Hold this, Julie." Bethany handed Julie the fire iron she was holding and rushed over to a closed bathroom door on the east side of the bathroom. She eased the door open, peeked into an old-fashioned bathroom covered with soft green walls, and vanished. Seconds later, she reappeared with a green hand towel. "Here. Gentle now." Bethany placed the hand towel over Davy's wound.

While Bethany tended to Davy's wound, Julie pulled herself together to think. She hurried over to the only window in the bedroom and, using extreme caution, peeled back a deep green drape just enough to see a beautiful clear lake surrounded by lush autumn woods.

"I see no one in the backyard area or near the lake," she called out to Bethany as her eyes scanned a land covered with bright autumn leaves.

"Hold the hand towel over your head. I'll be right back." Bethany ran over to Julie and joined her friend. The land in the back of the house was silent except for a stiff wind whispering about. The lake showed no signs of human interference, and the woods appeared to be filled with shadows rather than human life. "It takes an hour to reach the bottom of the mountain by car, and a half hour to reach town. I feel like I'm back on top of Icy Mountain."

"Me, too," Julie whispered. "Bethany...are we cursed?"

"I don't know," Bethany offered an honest answer, her heart taking a quick dive into a pessimistic pool of despair. *Maybe Julie and I are cursed? Three murder cases, and we're not even settled in Snow Falls yet. Well, we're not broken in, is more like it. But this is no time to worry whether or not you're cursed. I know I'm not Sarah Spencer. Sarah is a brilliant detective, but Sarah isn't here, and I must rely on my own wits.* "Okay, Julie, honey, we better get away from this window. Someone out there has a rifle, and I'll bet my bottom dollar whoever shot up Davy's cab is watching the house as we speak."

Julie quickly backed away from the window. The idea of being shot wasn't very appealing.

"Davy," she spoke in her thick British accent that became heavier with fear. "The phone is dead. Bethany believes the phone line has been cut."

"I wouldn't doubt it." Davy closed his eyes for a few seconds to gather his thoughts. "Why would someone leave a dead body out in the open?"

"To be found," Bethany answered Davy. "Why someone wanted the body to be found is a different question."

"What is this? Some kind of sick game?" Davy felt anger swell up inside of him. He threw his eyes at Bethany. "Look, I know it's none of my business, and Mrs. Lights, your mother, told me you two were coming to Old Wolf Mountain to take a vacation. But now I'm thinking there's more to this situation. If I'm right, I'd appreciate some open honesty here."

"Fair enough," Julie spoke before Bethany could. "Davy, two weeks ago I received a threatening phone call. I told Bethany about the phone call and my friend, bless her sweet soul, jumped into action, as you Americans might say. She pulled me out of our home in Snow Falls, Alaska as quickly as she could without making those we care for and love suspicious. Mrs. Lights, Bethany's mother, was being honest when she told you Bethany and I were traveling to your state to take a well-needed rest. We need to rest...and hide."

"Who threatened you?" Davy asked, his temper simmering down.

"I didn't recognize the man who called me, but in my past, I ruined a man's career. As I told Bethany earlier, Davy, the man whose career I ruined, was the only enemy I ever made in my life." Julie paused. "I would assume the man whose career I ruined is now ready to collect his revenge on me."

"I would agree"—Bethany took back the fire iron Julie was

holding— "but how would anyone have known we were traveling to Old Wolf Mountain, Julie? Unless our cabin was bugged." *Maybe the cabin was bugged? Not impossible.* "All we know right now, as facts, is that a man is dead, and someone made sure Davy couldn't leave the mountain."

Julie looked at poor Davy. The man was trying to tend to his wound the best he could.

"Why would someone want you to stay on the mountain? Wouldn't it make sense to let you leave? The more people a killer must deal with, the more complicated the equation. At least that's how I see this matter in my mind. I mean, Davy, you're not involved with Bethany or myself. We barely know you...no offense."

"No offense taken." Davy allowed his eyes to focus on the dead man sitting in the rocking chair. "He looks young."

"Around twenty-five or so. His body is still warm," Bethany pointed out. "I suppose I should check his pockets. I doubt I'll find anything, but maybe the killer left a message?" *And that option isn't an impossibility, either. If Davy was prevented from leaving, that means he was detained for a reason.*

"Yeah, check the pockets," Davy agreed. "Julie, stand near the bedroom door. The floors in this house creak bad. If anyone tries to sneak up on us, you should be able to hear."

"Good idea, but I'll need this." Julie took the fire iron Bethany was holding back again. "Sorry, love, but I have a meaner swing than you."

"No need to apologize." Bethany bit down on her lower lip. *Here I go.* Without wasting another precious second, she walked forward and checked the pockets of the dead man. Davy watched as Julie perched herself beside the bedroom door.

"Anything?" Davy asked.

"Nothing so far. I checked the pants pocket. Now I will check the jacket pockets." *Whoever you are, I hope you can forgive me for being so intrusive. I certainly mean no disrespect.*

Bethany worked her hands through a set of fancy pockets attached to a very expensive suit jacket. The outside pockets were clean, but when she checked the inside pocket, her hand struck something. *Let's see what I found.* She carefully exposed a folded-up piece of paper. As she did, her nose caught a whiff of what smelled like cigarette smoke. *Whoever this man is, he was a smoker. I can smell cigarette smoke on his clothes—faint, but there. Yet, there are no cigarettes on his body. Also, I can't smell any cologne on him. I don't have the courage to lift his head and look at his face, but in time, I'm afraid that's a chore that must be done.*

"What did you find, love?" Julie asked in a low voice.

"I'm not sure." Bethany stepped away from the dead body and walked over to Davy. She unfolded a small piece of white paper. "'The dead can't talk.'" Bethany read the four simple words aloud, and then dropped her eyes. *Whoever left the dead body left an obvious message, too. Someone is playing a very sick and demented game.*

"Love?" Julie asked. "What does that mean?" She didn't want to accept the obvious and hoped her dear friend would present an explanation that would defeat her own.

"It means that whoever left the dead body for me to find left a clear message behind as well." Bethany handed Davy the piece of paper. "It's not impossible to break into this old house. This house isn't equipped with a high-tech security system. Your run-of-the-mill, everyday basic lock is all this house has to keep the bad guys out. But..." Bethany raised a set of confused eyes. "This house also isn't lined with a bunch of hidden hallways. What you see is what you get, which means that when Julie and I walked upstairs, the killer was already downstairs."

Davy could hear frustration mounting in Bethany's voice. "Look, we'll wait until it gets dark and then sneak out into the woods and work our way down the mountain. I was born and raised in these woods. I know my way around. Clover

River isn't too far from here. All we have to do is work our way east until we locate the river and follow the river down the mountain."

"Davy, if we step outside, we may get shot," Bethany pointed out. "I'm sure whoever is outside is prepared to deal with any escape plan we might create. Right now, I think it would be wise if we stay locked inside this bedroom."

"I agree with Bethany," Julie told Davy, trying her best to speak respectfully. Davy was a man, and it was a man's duty to take charge when a dangerous situation presented itself. His plan of escape was very potent, but Julie had no desire to step outside and risk being shot. For the time being, everyone was safe, and that's what mattered the most. "I think it would be safer for all of us if we stayed in this bedroom."

To Bethany's relief, Davy simply nodded. "Yeah, at least until it gets dark. But even then, even if we got outside, there's no telling what could happen. We don't even know how many people there are outside. Making a run for it might not be so smart."

Making a run for it may be our last option, Bethany feared, but didn't voice her thought.

chapter four

"Love," Julie spoke in a low whisper, "it's getting dark. We can't stay in this room forever. We need food. We can drink water from the bathroom sink, but it's been hours since we've eaten."

Bethany could feel the claws of darkness destroying the little daylight that bravely lingered outside. Her heart could always feel night arriving—slowly, like a hideous monster dripping down from the sky and rising from the ground like black, soulless marbles that would eventually form a hungry, hideous creature.

"I'm hungry, too, honey," she confessed. *I can feel my blood sugar dropping. I know I need something to eat, but it's too dangerous to leave this bedroom. No one even has a gun. But how much longer can we go without eating? I can feel myself getting shaky. If my blood sugar continues to drop, I won't be any good to anyone. I'll become a medical burden.*

"I have cookies and other snacks in my suitcase," Julie informed everyone as she stared at the bedroom window with desperate eyes. The bedroom she was standing in was growing darker by the second. Of course, it would have been easy to flip on a light switch, but Bethany had suggested keeping the lights off. Julie didn't welcome the suggestion with open arms, but deep down, she knew her friend had a practical reason for wanting to stand in the dark. "I can run to my room and get the cookies if you and Davy will watch me. It won't take but a minute."

Bethany locked her eyes on Davy, who was standing next to a lonely fireplace, lost in thought.

"Davy?"

"Huh?" Davy slowly turned his head. "What is it?"

Davy has been lost in thought for the last hour. I wonder what he's been thinking about.

"Julie has snacks in her suitcase. She wants to go get the snacks, and I admit, I could use something to eat. I feel my blood sugar dropping."

"Oh. Uh, well, if she hurries, I guess you and I can stand guard in the hallway." Davy walked his eyes around the bedroom—a spacious room that offered luxury and comfort. On any other day, he would simply flick up a light, start a cozy fire, settle down in front of the fireplace with a warm book, and fade away into a quiet night. But he knew he was trapped in an unpleasant situation that destroyed any hope of having a peaceful night. If only life were a warm book and a cozy fireplace.

"Okay, Julie. We'll need to hurry. It's getting dark. We need to keep the lights off. Go as quickly as you can." Bethany felt her heart pick up its pace. The idea of Julie leaving the bedroom scared her. The idea of being locked in the bedroom with a dead body wasn't so thrilling, either. *Mother will have a nervous breakdown when she discovers this awful nightmare. She's liable to sell the lake house and land, and leave the state of North Carolina. What a horrible mess.*

Julie braced herself. "Okay, love, you unlock the door. Davy, you step out into the hallway first and take the fireplace iron. Once you say the coast is clear, I'll run into my bedroom as fast as I can and grab my suitcase. I'll bring my suitcase back to this bedroom. No sense in trying to find a bunch of snacks in my bedroom alone."

"Sounds like a plan." Davy left his place beside the fireplace and walked over to Julie. He gratefully accepted the fireplace iron from her, tested its weight in his hand, and nodded.

"Okay, let's hurry."

Bethany drew in a deep breath, glanced toward a rocking chair holding a dead body, and eased over to the bedroom door.

"Okay," she whispered, placing a set of uneasy hands on an old deadbolt lock. "Everyone ready?" Julie and Davy nodded. Bethany drew in one more deep breath and bravely unlocked the bedroom door. Once the door was open, Davy stepped into a dark hallway like a daring solider.

"Well?" Julie whispered.

Davy narrowed his eyes as he searched for any signs of danger. "I don't see anyone," he whispered back. "It's go time. Hurry."

Julie took off like a bolt of lightning without wasting a second. Bethany rushed out into the hallway behind her and joined Davy. "I want our eyes to get used to the dark. If we can't see them, they can't see us. At least that's what I'm hoping. The longer we stand in the dark, the more our eyes will become accustomed."

"That's what I thought your plan was," Davy whispered, stepping closer to Julie's bedroom. "Hurry," he called through an open bedroom door.

Julie knew exactly where her suitcases were. She moved toward an enormous bed, located two sleepy suitcases, grabbed both, and hightailed it back into the hallway.

"Whew, I was afraid someone might have been waiting for me in the bedroom."

"All the windows are nailed shut." Bethany had pointed out

that fact earlier, but reminded her friend to offer some form of comfort. "There's no hidden hallways or secret passages in this house. The only way into your bedroom is down this hallway, and you can hear how bad the floors creak under our feet."

Davy gazed down the hallway. He sure didn't like feeling like a trapped mouse. "Let's get back into the bedroom where it's safe."

"I would rather go outside and make a wild run for it," Julie confessed, her voice trembling. "I feel like all we're doing is waiting to be killed."

"I know how you feel," Bethany spoke in a low, troubled voice. "I'm just wondering why we weren't killed the moment we arrived. And why was Davy allowed to live? Two plus two is equaling five here, and I can't figure out why."

"Come on, back in the bedroom." Davy said. He quickly closed the bedroom door with a fast hand. "I don't know what's going on here, but I'm of the mind that it's better to stay in a foxhole rather than running out into an open field."

"Were you in the military?" Julie asked Davy.

Davy shook his head. "I wasn't, but my brother was. He was an infantry soldier for a couple of years, but on his twenty-second birthday he took part in a bad night jump. Busted up his right leg beyond repair."

"I'm sorry to hear that," Julie said genuinely.

"Yeah. John has never been the same. He took to drinking for a few years. He met his wife at a rehab center. They married. Julia became a teacher. She's on the school board now, and John started a cab business. He does okay...better than I'm doing."

Julie placed the suitcase she was holding onto a shadowy bed. "You shouldn't be so hard on yourself."

"Julie is right, Davy," Bethany agreed. "Divorce is a hideous monster to wrestle with."

Davy dropped his shoulders. His life was a deflated balloon, and he knew it. "Well, the damage is done. I lost everything. My home. My business, my truck. Now I'm a middle-aged man living in a garage apartment and driving a cab."

"You don't have to drive a cab. You told us you're a certified, skilled electrician. I'm sure there is plenty of work—"

"There is," Davy cut Bethany off as Julie dug a bag full of snacks out of her suitcase. "I can get work anywhere. The truth is, Bethany, I'm too tired to care. I've been my own boss for close to twenty years. I can't imagine going to work for a company that...well, I'm just not the type of guy who can work for another guy."

"Why not start you a new business?" Bethany asked. "It's not impossible."

"No, not impossible. And to be blunt, the skunk my ex-wife sold my business to will take a hard nosedive real soon. I could start my business again when I have some money. My ex-wife took everything from me, Bethany. The judge who took her case was a real slime bucket...an atheist, who hated me for my Christian views. My ex-wife poured out a river of crocodile tears while the man she left me for— some sleazy lawyer—ran my name into the mud and made everyone in the courtroom believe I was an abusive monster. Long story short, because everything I owned was in both my name and my ex-wife's name..." Davy sighed. "If only I knew that all these years, she was scheming to destroy me."

"I'm sorry, Davy. I can't imagine how angry and hurt you must feel." Bethany felt the words she spoke were pointless and filled with dead weight. *What can I say to a man who walks around with a knife stuck between his shoulder blades? I don't know Davy's entire story, but it's clear he is a man who was attacked and betrayed by a woman who was supposed to be a loving, faithful wife.*

"There's really no sense in thinking about it," Davy told Bethany. "What's done is done. Right now, we need to focus on getting off Old Wolf Mountain alive. Julie, how are you coming along with those snacks? I'm a bit hungry myself."

Julie fished out three packs of chocolate cookies from a paper bag filled with goodies.

"Here, everyone, have some cookies."

Bethany gratefully accepted a pack of cookies and tore in. *Julie and Amanda are as different as night and day in the character department, but in the stomach department, those two are twins. Must be a British thing. Not that I'm complaining.*

"These are very good. Thank you, Julie."

Davy took his pack of cookies and ate. "Bethany, for the last hour, I've been thinking about how we could get down the mountain without being seen. I don't know how many people might be outside…or even inside the house. The only solution I have is the Old Wolf trail."

"Old Wolf trail?" Julie asked as she munched her cookie.

Bethany glanced toward the bedroom window. There were perhaps ten minutes of weak daylight left outside, then the darkness of night would prevail. *The mountains grow so dark, the darkest dark I've ever seen in my life. When I was a little girl, I was always afraid of the nighttime, at least up on the mountain. The daylight hours were always so joyful and fun, but when night arrived, it felt as if the mountain transformed into a nightmare. I have no desire to go out into the night, but right now, the night may be our only escape.*

"What about the trail, Davy?" she asked, keeping her voice low.

"The trail leads east straight toward Clover River. I don't even know if the trail is still there. I remember seeing the trail on a map hanging on the living room wall downstairs. Your mother told me your great-grandfather cleared the trail—"

"Davy, that old trail hasn't been used since I was a little girl. It's probably so overgrown by now—"

Davy held up a quick hand, prompting Bethany to stop talking and pay attention. "Maybe so, but the trail leads to the river. We can use the cover of darkness to get to the river and then work our way south."

Before Bethany could whisper another word, Davy hurried over to her. "Someone could be listening to our every word...play along," he whispered in Bethany's ear. "Tell Julie."

Bethany looked into Davy's shadowy face and passed the message to Julie. "Alright, Davy, if we can get to the trail, it might be very difficult. The trail hasn't been used in years...and who knows how many people might be waiting outside?"

"Well, it might be more dangerous to wait in this bedroom," Julie pointed out.

What is Davy up to? He's obviously not a stupid man. No, Davy is a very intelligent man with a solid head sitting on his shoulders. "How would we ever get outside?" Bethany asked.

Davy felt relief touch his chest. He did not know who was inside the house or who was waiting outside in the darkness. All Davy knew was that he was responsible for protecting two innocent women in a world of trouble.

"We have to get to the basement. There's an old tunnel in the basement that used to be used as an underground railroad to help slaves escape."

Bethany wasn't aware of any such tunnel, but she wasn't about to throw cold water onto Davy's face. "Davy, that tunnel has been closed off for decades."

"It's our only chance of escape," Davy pointed out, grateful Bethany was playing along. "We'll wait until around midnight, and then we'll have to figure out how to get down to the basement without being seen. That's going to be the tricky part."

"Anything is better than standing in this bedroom with a dead body," Julie told Bethany as she munched another cookie. "If there's one dead body, there's bound to be more...and Bethany, love, I don't want to be part of a body count."

"Neither do I, honey." Bethany watched as the last of the daylight dissipated. A cruel, black darkness gripped the bedroom and grinned. Night had arrived. *What is Davy's plan? And what is my plan if Davy's plan fails? I don't have a clue. All I know is that a man is dead, and I'm trapped in this bedroom. Who is outside? Who is behind this? Is there more than one person? There are too many unknown variables. I hope whatever plan Davy is thinking up will be better than my own, because right now, all I can think to do is make a wild run for it under the cover of night.*

Outside in the darkness, two men eyed a dark house. "We can't let them leave here alive," one man spoke viciously. "They have to die."

"We'll kill them, don't worry. Right now, just calm down and relax. We have our prey exactly where we want them and we're listening to every word they say."

"What if they try to get to the basement—" the first man objected.

"Don't worry. They're not going anywhere. I know the house and the land better than I know myself. Our prey isn't going anywhere...not alive, anyway. After we get what we want, we'll make sure our prey ends up dead."

chapter five

D avy nodded toward a sleepy, lonely fireplace. "We're
going to spider-walk up the fireplace and then use the
roof to escape," he whispered in Bethany's ear.

The sound of cold, howling winds scratched at the
bedroom window. Usually, Bethany worried when the winds
grew stronger during the night; however, the power inserting
itself into the chilly winds outside was a blessing in disguise.

Bethany walked over to the fireplace and bent down. How
long had it been since she had stepped into her parents' old
bedroom? Years upon years, it felt like. How long had it been
since a fire had given the fireplace any signs of life? Years?
Bethany believed so. It wasn't often that her family used the
house.

Using her left hand, she felt a cold stone floor. *Can Julie
and I crawl up this fireplace? This seems so impossible. We don't
even know if our voices are being listened to. I would rather err on
the side of caution, even so, I feel so trapped. I'm far too old to climb
up an unstable fireplace. Even if we make it to the roof, then what?
Surely the bedroom is being watched from the outside.*

"Love?" a voice whispered.

Bethany turned her head, seeing Julie squat down beside

her. "There has to be another way," she whispered so low that her voice barely carried into Julie's sharp ears.

"There isn't."

Bethany glanced to her right and spotted Davy bending down next to her ear. "What will we do even if we get up onto the roof?" she whispered. "The roof is full of sharp—"

"Bethany, if we can get up onto the roof"—Davy nodded upward—"you hear the rain. It's raining hard. The rain is supposed to change over to wintry mix by midnight and then eventually into snow. You feel how cold this bedroom is getting. The temperature outside is dropping at a good pace. We have to get up to the roof and use the fire escape your mother showed me."

Fire escape? I'm not aware of any fire escape. Bethany stared into Davy's face with confused eyes. Was there an actual fire escape she wasn't aware of? *It's been so many years since I've been to this house. Mother mentioned making a few improvements in a letter once. Could she have added a fire escape? It's possible. Mother is a woman who prides herself on being active.*

"Alright, Davy, the ball is in your court," Bethany said. "We'll do what you say."

"Good." Davy dropped onto all fours and crawled into the fireplace. "Julie," he whispered, "you'll go up first, Bethany second, and me last. When you get to the roof, just hunker down until I get up there." Davy flung his eyes upward and studied a dark tunnel. "The fire escape is just off the bedroom window to the right. The roof is very steep, so we must work as a team to create a chain. It's going to be very tedious, but if we're careful, we should be able to escape."

"What if someone is watching?" Bethany worried. "We could be shot like ducks."

"Julie, it's raining cats and dogs outside. This weather might prove to be a blessing because whoever crippled my cab will be standing outside in this weather. We're trapped—and I think that's the point. Someone wanted to trap us in this house. I don't think anyone will be watching the roof right now. Also, you said it yourself, the windows are nailed shut. I've been thinking about that. If I were trying to trap someone, I would worry about the windows, but obviously the windows aren't a great concern, right?" Davy whispered. "You can't even see the fire escape unless you break the main window and look out to your right. I should know, because I was working on the generators when the man who installed the fire escape was here."

Bethany closed her eyes. She could appreciate that Davy was trying to think on his feet, but his escape plan seemed perilous. What if someone fell off the roof or slipped while climbing up the fireplace, then crashed down and broke a leg?

She didn't want to make the situation any more difficult than what it was. *What to do? Agree with Davy or try to think of another plan? So far, my ideas have come up flat.*

Before Bethany could speak, a loud, booming voice that seemed to crash through a megaphone exploded into the bedroom.

"Listen up! You're trapped! There's more of us than you! I have people outside and inside. If you try to escape, you'll be shot on sight, and that means trying to escape to the basement as well! Stay where you are until you receive further instructions! And just to show you I'm serious—"

A deadly, sharp bullet crashed through the top of the bedroom window, ripped through a heavy drape, raced across the bedroom, and lodged itself into the top of the bedroom door. Davy grabbed Bethany and Julie and pulled them down onto the floor as low as he could.

"That was a warning!" the voice yelled. "Stay in the bedroom until you hear from me again!"

"Davy, do you recognize that voice?" Bethany asked, frantic. "The voice seems to be coming from the bottom of the staircase and—"

"No...but he's a local. I can tell by his accent. He has a

thick North Carolinian Mountain accent like I do, only my accent isn't as thick," Davy whispered back.

"That voice doesn't belong to the man who called and threatened me," Julie added. "The man who called me had a London accent."

Maybe the man who called Julie hired a few locals to do his bidding? Bethany felt her mind race. *Okay. I have to stay calm and think, just like I did on Ice Mountain. Nothing has changed. If I panic, I'll let fear defeat me. I have to think and figure out what is happening. So let's review the facts real quick: a dead man appears to be in his mid-twenties, Davy's cab was crippled and he was allowed to return to the house alive, and now we're trapped in this bedroom. A man who sounds like a local has just ordered everyone to stay in the bedroom and sent a bullet as a warning. Julie said the voice of the man who called her doesn't match the voice of the man downstairs—those are the facts. But wait...the man who yelled at us said not to try and get to the basement, so that must mean the bedroom is bugged. Maybe it's time to use that fact to our advantage?*

"Davy—"

"I know, botch the fireplace plan," Davy groaned under his breath.

"Listen, we know someone outside watched the bedroom window, and we know there's someone downstairs," Bethany whispered. "We're trapped in this bedroom, but that doesn't mean we're without hope."

"I'm all ears, love," Julie spoke low enough for her voice to avoid the listening device attached to the back of an antique lamp on a table beside the main bed.

"No one has come upstairs...yet. We received a warning."

"The bullet that was shot into the bedroom was shot high, too," Davy quickly pointed out. "Whoever is outside deliberately shot high to make sure no one was hit."

"And that could mean that the person who yelled up at us from downstairs—at least he sounded like he was standing at the bottom of the staircase—might not have been being as truthful as we think? Why stay downstairs? Why hold back? If we're outnumbered, why not simply take us by force?" As Bethany whispered, new questions full of life and urgency formed in her mind. *Why haven't we been taken by force yet? And why leave a dead body in the bedroom? Why leave an ugly message attached to the dead body? Someone is playing a sick game, but there's a hidden purpose to the game designed to benefit the killer—or killers. But how are Julie and I connected to the game? Did the man who called and threatened Julie hire a bunch of local yo-yos to bully us into a corner?*

"Julie, Davy, any ideas?"

"No, love. I'm very confused about all this," Julie confessed. "I don't mean to sound like a dim bulb, but I don't have the faintest as to what is going on. I think it would be easier for me to figure out how to scale the walls of Buckingham Palace blindfolded than to figure out the danger we're in."

"All I know is that the man who hollered up at us sounded local, and the person who sent that bullet through the window knew how to shoot," Davy whispered, and gently shook his head. "The rifle that shot that bullet didn't sound like an expensive high-powered rifle...more like a cheap hunting rifle. Maybe a Remington 783 .243 Win...or a CVA Scout .450 Bushmaster?"

"You know your rifles good," Bethany told Davy.

"I was an avid hunter once," Davy explained, keeping his voice low. "I've hunted with many rifles through my years. I stopped hunting last year. Lost the heart for it. That doesn't mean I can't identify a rifle when I hear it. The rifle we heard was close and sounded cheap."

Bethany turned her head and scanned a very dark bedroom that her eyes had adjusted to. By keeping the lights off, her plan to allow everyone's eyes to adjust to the dark had paid off—or so Bethany hoped.

What would Sarah do? Well, Sarah would have her gun on her and...and, wait a minute, a gun? A gun? Mother always demanded Daddy keep guns out of the house...oh, how could I have been so dumb? Daddy's old gun!

"Davy, Julie, follow me and stay quiet!" Bethany's urgent tone told Julie and Davy to act without asking questions.

Bethany raced across the bedroom and dived under the main bed.

"Oh, be here, please be here," Bethany begged as she felt the underside of the bed with frantic hands. "Be here, be here...oh Daddy, please tell me you never got rid of that old gun of yours..." Bethany forced her hands to explore the bottom of the bed quickly, feeling as if she were suddenly locked in a dark cave. "Be here...be…"

Bethany's right hand struck a strange wooden box attached to the underside of the bed. The underside of the bed was made from a heavy walnut wood. The box was nailed to the wood with small nails.

"This is it...it has to be."

She drew in a deep breath of dusty cold air and fiddled with the box, finding a closed lid attached to it. With a careful hand, she eased the lid open and inserted her hand into the box.

"The gun...oh Daddy, bless you for not listening to mother when she fussed at you to get rid of your gun."

Bethany cautiously retrieved a 1980 Smith and Wesson revolver that, she feared, was full of rusted bullets. Bethany did not know how long bullets were good for. She was going to find out.

"Love, what are you doing?" Julie asked as soon as she saw Bethany crawl out from under the bed.

Bethany placed her left finger over her lips and then held up her right hand. Julie and Davy moved forward until they spotted the gun Bethany was holding.

"Take it," Bethany whispered to Davy. Davy nodded, took

the gun, and using skilled hands, checked to see if the gun was loaded. Bethany and Julie waited. Davy offered a quick nod that confirmed the gun was loaded.

Well, at least we're armed. That's a start.

"What now?" Julie asked, hoping she was speaking in a low enough whisper to avoid being heard by deadly ears.

"Well," Bethany suddenly raised her voice to an audible level. "We were given instructions to remain in the bedroom. We have time. We need to figure out how to get to the basement and find the escape tunnel."

Julie bit her lower lip for a second, and decided it was time to think instead of panic.

"It'll be impossible to get to the basement now. Someone will be watching, Bethany."

"I agree," Davy chimed in. "We need a new escape plan. The question is, how are we going to escape? Someone is downstairs and someone is outside." He allowed anger and frustration to enter his voice. "I wish I knew who was behind this. I don't enjoy being pushed into a corner."

"Julie, could it be that the man who called and threatened you is behind this?" Bethany asked somewhat desperately. "Did you recognize the voice who ordered us to stay upstairs?"

Instead of offering an honest answer, Julie knew what Bethany was fishing for. "I don't know. The voice I heard on the phone and the voice that ordered us to stay where we are, it could have been the same voice. I don't know. Maybe?"

We must keep our aggressors guessing as much as possible while we try to create an escape plan. The only problem is, Davy is right. We have a killer downstairs and a killer outside. For the moment, we're trapped. No one knows how many people are downstairs or outside. One...two...ten...twenty? Even if there is just one person downstairs and one person outside, they are obviously armed and willing to kill. We can't take that chance. Also, I believe we're being kept alive because there's a hidden agenda. The killers want something, I'm sure of that now. But what do they want? And why did they let Davy live instead of killing him?

"Julie, got any more cookies? I'm feeling shaky again."

"Of course, love." Julie hurried to get her dear friend some cookies from the bag of goodies sitting on the bed.

"I've got to use the bathroom. I'll hurry." Without saying another word, Davy hurried into the bathroom attached to the bedroom and closed a heavy door.

He went to check the gun. In the meantime, I need to think.

"Love," Julie whispered, dropping her voice to a minimal whisper again as she handed Bethany a pack of cookies. "Maybe...maybe Davy's ex-wife hasn't pulled her claws out of him just yet. Maybe this isn't about us."

Bethany gazed at the darkness shrouding the room and looked at Julie. *Maybe Julie just struck gold. We're certainly going to find out one way or another.*

chapter six

Sheriff Riley Murphy grumbled to himself as he forced an old clunker of a car—a 1983 Oldsmobile, to be exact—up a winding mountain road being pounded by a dangerous storm. Rachel Lights, the dear mother of Bethany Lights, had called and insisted that Riley drive all the way to the top of Old Wolf Mountain and check on her daughter to make sure the built-in generators Davy had installed were working properly and to discover why the phones weren't working.

Rachel was very upset that the phone line connected to the lake house was out. Usually, Riley would have told dear old Rachel Lights to shove her request into a bean can, but the truth was, Rachel tossed heavy money into the pocket of a run-down sheriff's office—and it wasn't as if the woman constantly called and demanded favors. In fact, Riley couldn't remember the last time he had spoken to Rachel in person other than a simple hello at some function he couldn't recall. It wouldn't have been proper to turn down the request of a worried mother. In fact, Riley knew, to tell Rachel Lights to cram her request into a bean can would have been downright rude—and Riley Murphy wasn't a rude man. Tough as nails, mean as cat snot, grumpier than a hungry grizzly bear, sure, but rude? No.

"Come on, ol' tiger, you can make it up this mountain..." Riley reached out his left hand, patted a sun-scarred dash, and focused back on the road.

A hard wind fell across the old gravel road Riley was driving up, rocking the Oldsmobile with a violent hand. Riley eased off a worn-down gas pedal and let the wind pass. Only hard, icy rain littered the headlights stretching out in front of his car. Thick darkness stood on both sides of the road like black marble guardians preparing to slaughter anyone who dared to venture up the mountain road.

"This storm probably caused a tree to fall and knock out the phone line up at the old lake house. Bethany Lights is probably sitting in front of a warm fire sipping on coffee, and here I am risking my backside driving up this old road." Riley ran a hard hand through a head of thick gray hair. Even though he was only forty-five years old, he had grayed early in life.

Riley's life had started out pretty good. He grew up in a solid Christian family, played high school football, went off to college, and eventually earned his private pilot's license and joined the navy at twenty-three. He worked hard and earned his flying wings for the navy. But at the age of thirty, disaster struck when a transport plane Riley was flying suffered a serious malfunction. Riley and his co-pilot, a good friend who called himself Tomcat, attempted to carry out an emergency landing but couldn't handle the plane. The plane lost all power and took a serious dive, crashing down into a field northeast of Pensacola.

Riley was busted up badly. His co-pilot died on impact along with three other crew members. After the crash, Riley spent months in a hospital recovering and was eventually let loose from the navy on a medical discharge. He returned home to Pine Lakes, North Carolina, defeated and angry. His father, who was sheriff at the time, talked his son into becoming a deputy sheriff. Because Riley could no longer fly, for personal reasons, he agreed to pursue a new career in law enforcement. At forty, he took his father's place as sheriff. "Yeah, that's my life story. A lousy story," Riley grunted as he drove.

"Sheriff?" a broken voice came through a rusted old CB radio sitting on the passenger seat like a nagging wife.

Riley glanced toward the CB radio with eyes that suddenly felt weary instead of grumpy. Donald Haymore, a young, ambitious deputy, was pulling the night shift and reviewing all the cold case files—out of boredom more than curiosity. Riley shook his head and reluctantly grabbed the CB radio microphone.

"What is it, Donald? I can barely read you. I'm halfway up the old mountain road."

"Just got a call, sheriff. A woman who called herself Wanda Brakemyer said her husband, some guy named Patrick, came to Pine Lakes two days ago and hasn't contacted her since. She wants to put in a missing person report."

"Oh, for the love of everything good." Riley gritted his teeth.

Far away, a young deputy leaned back in a wooden desk chair and flinched. Making Riley Murphy mad wasn't a good idea. Riley reminded Donald Haymore of the Incredible Hulk wearing the face of John Wayne. Riley wasn't built like a massive body builder—he was normal in size—but the man's temper was massive.

"Mrs. Brakemyer said she's driving to the station to file the report. I thought you should know."

"Yeah, just fill out the report." Riley slowed the Oldsmobile to a stop. "Listen, Donald, don't make a mountain out of an ant hill, do you hear me? Just get the needed information and put the report on my desk. Is that clear?" He knew Donald had a tendency to call out the prison dogs anytime someone simply jaywalked. The guy was worse than Barney Fife.

"I will, sheriff. You can count on me!" Donald promised.

Riley let out a miserable groan. "Just do your job, son," he ordered. "Is there anything else?"

"Uh, well, Mrs. Brakemyer said she and her husband are newlyweds, married a month ago. She sounded about my age, twenty-five or so. Seemed kind of strange to me that a newly married man would leave his wife and come to Pine Lakes. She also said she and her husband are from New York. She had a real thick New York accent."

Donald's voice broke a few times, but Riley could catch most words with a trained ear as heavy, icy rain battered the Oldsmobile. As much as Riley hated to admit it, the situation in question seemed a little strange. Why would a young married kid from New York travel to Pine Lakes two weeks after he got married? Pines Lakes was a small family community. Sure, occasionally, drugs reared up like filthy litter, but Riley cleaned out the trash with a harsh, skilled hand. The only trouble Pine Lakes had had in the last five years since Riley had become sheriff was a green-eared drug dealer pushing cocaine and a few kids who decided breaking into people's summer homes might be fun. Otherwise, most of the crime consisted of speeding tickets, a drunk driver or two, and a couple of domestic disputes. Nothing major.

"Alright, Donald, get the lady's information. I'll be back to the station as soon as I can. I'll be a while."

"Yeah, it's a long way up to the top of Old Wolf Mountain, but don't worry, sheriff. I have everything under control here at the station. Everything is quiet as a mouse," Donald promised. "I was just going over the old Jones case and—"

"Son, Mr. Taylor Jones has been dead for ten years. His son lives in Des Moines. His daughter lives in Phoenix. The man's wife is living in an assisted living center in Flagstaff. What in the world do you expect to come up with?"

"Well, a man was killed, sheriff, and—"

"Winston Jones was an old man who got drunk and drowned in the river. Everyone knows that. His son, Taylor Jones, was suspected of murder because he was seen fighting with his old man before the drowning. Even if you could prove Taylor Jones killed his old man, the guy is a dead stiff. Get it?" Riley snapped.

"Oh...well, I guess that puts a damper on the case. Well, there's other cases."

Riley moaned. "Let me know if the world explodes. Sheriff out." Riley tossed down the CB radio microphone he was holding and got his Oldsmobile moving. "Somebody should have shot me for hiring that kid."

Bethany, Julie, and Davy weren't aware that the grumpy sheriff was on his way up to the lake house. For the time being, they were trapped in a dark bedroom struggling to create a plan.

"Davy, tell us more about your wife." Bethany hated to press a sore button, but if Julie's assumption was correct—if Davy's ex-wife was hiding behind a deadly curtain—it was prudent that Davy spill some beans.

Davy walked over to a green sitting couch and plopped down. His eyes had adjusted to the dark so well that he felt like his eyes had become the eyes of a prowling midnight cat.

"Tracy and I met in college. Freshman year. I was young and stupid. I fell for the first pretty face I saw." Davy lowered his eyes and examined the old gun he was gripping in his right hand. "Tracy sure was pretty...and she used her looks to break a lot of guys. I was just one guy in a thousand who dared to ask her out on a date. We went and saw a movie...can't remember what the movie was. After that, Tracy gave me the cold shoulder for a while and life went on."

Bethany allowed her mind to leave the trapped world she was standing in to enter a warm, breezy college campus with lovely manicured lawns and towering, aged buildings filled with voices from an age long forgotten. She spotted a young, handsome, nineteen-year-old kid carrying a backpack crammed with books and rushing to one class or another.

"What brought you back into contact with Tracy Bates?" she asked Davy.

Davy leaned back on the couch. He knew his every word spoken above a whisper would be overheard. He didn't care.

"I'm not really sure, to be honest," he confessed. "I left Professor Mulgrew's class one autumn afternoon and bumped right into Tracy as she was walking by. Tracy didn't even recognize me. Anyway, to make a long story short, I was in a bad mood that afternoon because I was fuming over a grade I got on a major test. Instead of apologizing to Tracy, I chewed her head off, told her to take a long hike off a short cliff, and stormed off. The next day I went to the library to get some study time in, and Tracy showed up...and from that day forward, she and I became what people called an item."

"And you two dated all the way through college?" Bethany asked.

"We did, and we married right after we graduated. I graduated with a degree in electrical engineering. Tracy got her degree in education." Davy shook his head. "I was offered a lot of good jobs, but...well, Bethany, Julie, I'm a hometown boy. Tracy begged me to move to New York, but I couldn't imagine living in a big, smelly concrete city. I need grass and trees and fresh air. I'm not the type of guy who gets excited about riding on a crime-filled subway each day. When I told Tracy we were going to settle down in Pine Lakes, we had a real terrible argument, and that almost ended our marriage."

"What happened?" Julie spoke up, authentically curious about Davy's past.

"My dad died," Davy explained in a voice that dove into a painful sea of memories. "My dad was at work, and he had a brain aneurysm erupt. No one even knew, not even me. Dad was sixty-eight. He and mom had me and my brother late in life. Anyway, when dad died, I told Tracy to either take a walk or move to Pine Lakes. My mother needed me, and I wasn't going to turn my back on her."

"And Tracy Bates agreed?" Bethany asked.

Davy sat silent for a minute before answering. "Bethany, to be honest, I don't think Tracy had a choice. Tracy's parents were divorced while we were in college. Her mother moved to Los Angeles and her dad—whom Tracy claims was a worthless bag of sand—moved to San Diego. Tracy never talked about her parents much. Her parents didn't even show up at her graduation. I think her past has a lot to do with the way she was, why she always attempted to manipulate people, keep people at a distance, that kind of thing. When my dad died, I put my foot down and Tracy had a choice: leave me or move to Pine Lakes."

"And she chose Pine Lakes."

"And became a teacher at Pine Lakes Elementary School, and eventually became the principal," Davy finished for Bethany, adding in a sour voice, "By the time Tracy worked her way up the ladder, she was bitter as a cold-blooded scorpion. Our marriage failed years before we finally divorced. Why and how we stayed together for twenty years is beyond my understanding."

Bethany read something in Davy's voice that made her ask, "Tracy didn't remain as a principal for very long, did she?"

"No. A large group of parents got together and demanded her resignation after Tracy tried to push a lot of hateful ideologies into the school she was in charge of. The school board investigated, many teachers stood up and testified against Tracy, and within two weeks, she was canned," Davy explained. "That was about three years ago. Sure seems a lot longer."

Davy's ex-wife doesn't sound like a very pleasant woman. The woman sounds like a poisonous scorpion.

"Davy, did Tracy Bates stay in Pine Lakes after your divorce?"

"That's the strange part—she did," Davy confessed. "She took the house, my business, everything. Instead of leaving Pine Lakes, she stayed. Why? I have no idea. All I know is that she somehow got Judge Green dismissed from our divorce case and had some outside judge brought in. Because I pretty much know everyone in Pine Lakes and the surrounding area, Tracy's lawyer demanded that a judge who didn't know me be allowed to handle our divorce case."

"That loudmouth needs to shut up!" Brad Griffin snapped in a vicious voice. "I don't like him talking—"

"Let him run his mouth," Walley Griffin told his brother calmly. "Davy ain't hurting a thing. Besides, he may say something that might help us. So shut up, dry off, and listen instead of running your trap."

A hideous grin spread across Walley's face. He was a man on a mission, and by the time his mission was complete, there was going to be a lot of dead bodies lying around.

chapter seven

Could it be that Tracy Bates is behind this? If so, why? Why would she want to continue punishing an innocent man who seems defeated? What purpose would a woman have to punish an innocent man after she already obliterated his life? And why here? Why at the lake house? Tracy Bates could have struck anywhere, so why here at the lake house? And who is the dead man? Is the dead man somehow connected to Tracy Bates? Davy claims he doesn't recognize the dead man. And who is the man with the megaphone? And who was the man who put a bullet through the bedroom window? There's too many questions. I feel like Steve in Blue's Clues. *I have a clue, but we need to gather all three to figure out the clue.*

Bethany listened as cold water ran out of an antique faucet attached to an old porcelain bathroom sink. Standing in her parent's bathroom—a bathroom off-limits to her as a child—felt strange. *Oh Daddy, how I miss you. I wish you were here. You always helped me figure out the difficulties of life. Now I'm on my own, and the path is very hard.*

Julie eased open the bathroom door and stepped into a medium-sized bathroom that was fit for a king—at least in her eyes. The bathroom was considered merely acceptable in the eyes of Bethany's mother.

"Love," she whispered, closing the bathroom door, "I need to speak to you."

"Sure, honey."

"Davy is watching the bedroom door," Julie explained, allowing her voice to rise a little. "After talking about the spider he was married to, I think his mood has sunk to the floor."

"I believe so, too." Bethany bent down and gently splashed some cold water onto her face even though the bathroom air was very frigid. "I can still smell my daddy's aftershave lotion. Faint, but there. I guess mother never got rid of it. Mother claims to be a sensible woman, but deep down, she's just as sentimental as I am."

"It must be very difficult for you to be in this house," Julie whispered. "I've been wondering how you're feeling. I know we haven't known each other for many years, but I feel very close to you...like sisters. I can sense that being here is very hard for you."

Bethany turned off the cold-water faucet with a tired hand. "My parents stopped coming to the lake house when I was about seventeen. By then, I was preparing to go to college, and the trip to the lake house was very long and took a great deal of planning. Back in my youth, this house didn't have any built-in generators. Daddy had plenty of kerosene lanterns and candles about, and at night, he had fires going in every fireplace. That meant a lot of firewood was needed. Well, you get my point."

"I do," Julie nodded. She leaned back against a solid wood door and tried to relax as much as possible. "I'm exhausted, love, and starving. Cookies aren't filling my tummy. But my exhaustion and my hunger for actual food are going to have to wait."

"What's on your mind?" Bethany asked, turning to face Julie. Even though the bathroom was dark, she could make out Julie's appearance as if a bright candle was burning.

"I've been thinking about what Davy told us about his ex-wife. Love, I can't put my finger on the button, but I keep getting this odd feeling that somehow Tracy Bates is involved. Why?"

"Because Davy was left alive instead of killed, right?" Bethany asked.

"That's exactly it. I keep wondering why Davy was allowed to run back to the house. If he wasn't allowed to leave the mountain, then why wasn't he killed? It makes little sense unless someone Davy knows is involved. Well, Davy told us his parents are dead and that the only living relative he has in Pine Lakes is his brother." Julie spoke in a clear, direct tone that impressed Bethany.

"And his brother owns a cab business and is married to a woman who doesn't seem to be very fond of Davy," Bethany pointed out. "Seems like no one is fond of Davy."

"Love, you didn't grow up in Pine Lakes, did you?"

"No. I grew up in North Field, a town about fifty miles southeast of here, close to Raleigh. Davy lived in North Field when he went to high school because his parents needed to live close to Raleigh to be near Davy's doctors...at least that's what he told us. According to Davy, his parents moved back to the Pine Lakes community after he left for college." Bethany slowly folded her arms and leaned back against the bathroom sink. "I believe Davy is telling us the truth, Julie."

"So do I," Julie confirmed. "That's why I am wondering if Davy is being set up for murder?"

"That thought has crossed my mind, too." *Julie may appear like the quiet type, but she's a smart woman...very smart. She may have an appetite like Amanda, but I think she has a bigger appetite for mysteries. I'm sure glad she's on my side.* "What if we're wrong? What if Davy was left alive for another reason? I'm not trying to throw a monkey wrench in our theory—"

"But it is smart to think from many different angles. I understand, and I've considered that option." Julie reached into her coat pocket and pulled out a pack of cookies. "Cookie, love? Peanut butter chocolate."

"No thanks, honey. I'm craving a solid more than a sweet right now." Bethany drew in a deep breath. She could clearly smell her daddy's old shaving lotion. The scent nearly brought tears to her eyes. "Any ideas?"

"I was hoping you might go first. But before you do, I have a feeling you've been thinking about Tracy Bates just as much as I have."

"I have," Bethany admitted. "I've been wondering why a woman like Tracy Bates would want to remain in a small community like Pine Lakes after divorcing Davy. The only likely explanation my mind can reason with is—"

"Revenge," Julie answered for Bethany.

"The woman was fired from her job. According to Davy, the entire process was a very humiliating and infuriating experience for Tracy Bates. It could stand to reason that Tracy Bates is determined to get revenge. If that's the case, why would she involve us? Why attempt to imprison us in this house? Why let Davy leave? Why leave a dead body behind with a foul message?" Bethany let out a heavy, exhausted sigh. "There's numerous questions and no solid ground to stand on."

"Assumption is a terrible ground to stand on," Julie said. "But love, I think we might be on the right track. I can't explain why or how I know this."

"Gut feeling, huh?" Bethany asked.

"Well, yes," Julie admitted.

"Okay, honey, let's stay on this track for now before we consider other possibilities." Bethany prepared for a long talk with her new friend—a friend who was now closer than a real sister. "What if Tracy Bates is attacking Davy? Let's assume that Tracy Bates wants to set Davy up for murder. That leaves us with the dead body."

"Well, love, Davy said his wife left him for a sleazy

lawyer," Julie pointed out. "The dead man in the bedroom looks like some person you would see walking around Brooklyn at midnight."

"Okay, let's assume there's a connection. But why here? Why the lake house?" Bethany asked, grateful that Julie was at her side. *I have a sister now, and we're going to make a great team...we* do *make a great team. I hope someday, we will find love again, meet two wonderful men, get married...the idea of love isn't impossible. But for now, Julie and I are running solo—two gals against the world.*

"Love, was your mother part of the school board that canned Tracy Bates?" Julie asked.

"I..." Bethany stopped in her tracks. *That's one question that never entered my mind. Julie is brilliant!* "No, my mother was never part of the school board, but my family donates a lot of money to the Pine Lakes community. Also to the sheriff's office, the senior citizen center, and especially the schools. Julie, I never connected those dots!"

Julie heard excitement enter Bethany's voice. "I'm not Sherlock Holmes, love. My mind was just wandering around a lot of confusing rooms filled with uncertain questions."

Bethany bit down on her lip. "Could my mother somehow be involved, Julie? Mother never tells me about her personal business. That's not her way, and it's not ladylike to speak of personal business matters that don't involve a person directly. Mother was—still is—a private woman. That's the way she was raised to be."

"Well, love, is that so bad? For a woman to honor the old ways of life instead of being a busy gossip? Your mother isn't exactly a horrible monster. In fact, love, I found her to be very endearing and loving. Yes, she's a tad stuffy, but your mother wasn't raised to express her inner emotions on a dime, love. I kind of feel you and your mother have a lot in common. At times, it takes a hammer and a pair of pliers to get you to smile...and at other times, I notice a tear can fall freely."

"I suppose my mother and I do have a few things in common. I take mostly after Daddy. Daddy was a free-spirited man who loved to laugh." Bethany drew in a deep breath of cold air. The memory of her daddy whispered into her heart like a fresh morning rose sitting on a tall mountain top. "If Daddy were here, he would probably tell me to focus on the facts and set emotion aside. I suppose he would be right...and that means I have to think of my mother from a practical point of view."

"Okay, let's do that," Julie agreed. "Let's assume that your mother was involved in the termination of Tracy Bates."

"Well, mother doesn't sit on the school board, but she donates quite a bit of money to the schools in Pine Lakes. That means she most likely would have caught wind of any foul birds flying around...like Tracy Bates." Bethany grew silent for a minute and allowed her thoughts to wander around a few possible logical and practical possibilities. "Mother is a Christian woman who has fought to keep Christian values in the schools in Pine Lakes and the surrounding communities. A woman like Tracy Bates would have ruffled her feathers."

"Which means it's almost certain Mrs. Lights, your dear mother, knew about Tracy Bates," Julie added.

"Yes, that train of thought seems practical," Bethany admitted. *Could it be that Julie struck gold? Julie certainly is a brilliant woman in my eyes. I think she's stumbled into a gold mine that we need to continue exploring.* "Julie—"

A quick hand tapped the bathroom door before Bethany could continue. "I hear someone coming up the stairs!" Davy called out in an urgent tone.

"Oh dear." Bethany ran to Julie. Julie snatched the bathroom door open and hurried back into the bedroom as Davy ran to the bedroom door. It didn't take but a second to hear the heavy footsteps sneaking up the staircase. Each stair creaked and moaned like a dying coyote. "Davy—"

"I'm ready," Davy assured Bethany.

Bethany and Julie hurried to Davy, who checked the gun he was holding and waited. "If any shooting starts, you two get up that fireplace," he whispered. "That's not a request, either."

Bethany looked at Julie. Julie drew in a nervous breath and waited. "You, in the bedroom," a voice hollered, "listen up!"

"That's not the same voice as before," Julie quickly pointed out.

"No, it isn't," Bethany agreed.

"We're listening! What is it?" Davy yelled through the closed bedroom door.

"If you want to live, do like I say!" Brad Griffin barked. "My brother is outside, so I have to make this quick. Just do like you're told and I'll make sure you live! I'm playing the game really good—and if you're smart, so will you. All I want is the money! I didn't kill that fella in the bedroom and I ain't going down for murder! Get it?"

"What's this all about?" Davy demanded.

"Just play the game and do what you're told!" Brad hollered. "I ain't stupid! But let me tell you something, boy, my brother ain't stupid, either. He ain't gonna let anyone leave this house alive, including me. So stop running your trap and do what you're told. I'll step in when I can and save you...but so help me, if you don't tell me where the money is, I will go to prison for murder!"

"What money? What are you talking about—"

"Don't play stupid, boy!" Brad gritted his teeth so hard he nearly chipped a tooth. "My brother knows all about the money! Play smart or die! I gotta get back downstairs. You've been warned!"

Brad glanced down the staircase to make sure his brother wasn't anywhere around. Yes, for the time being, he was playing the part of a money-hungry killer, but it was Walley

Griffin who was the actual killer...and Walley was only a puppet being controlled by a very cruel puppet master. Brad wasn't about to take the fall for a murder he didn't commit. No, Brad had his sights set on some buried treasure that was going to set him up for life. A nice tropical island and a pocket full of money sounded real nice.

"Play smart!" Brad yelled, and then rushed back downstairs to wait for his brother to return from the storm. Where Walley had gone, Brad had no idea.

Davy turned to Bethany and Julie wearing a confused expression. "What in the world is going on here?" he demanded as if the two women standing in front of him had all the answers.

"Money?" Bethany answered Davy's question with a question. "What money?"

"Well, love," Julie spoke in a voice that nearly hit the floor, "looks like we've just had another ugly question mark added to this awful riddle we're trapped in." She bowed her head and let out a heavy, exhausted sigh. "The next time we decide to leave Snow Falls, lock me in our cabin, love, and never let me leave."

chapter eight

"We've got company!" Walley Griffin grabbed the sleeve of a greasy brown coat and shoved his brother into a large foyer. "Sheriff is on his way up!"

"Sheriff Murphy? How do you know that?" Brad asked.

Walley stared into a youthful face that resembled the perfect mountain hillbilly. Brad Griffin was a 27-year-old high school dropout who spent his time changing tires at a rundown tire service center in Raleigh. Black teeth from years of neglect and chewing tobacco complemented Brad's rough, dumb face. A mop of messy brown hair sitting under a camouflage hunting cap completed the full costume.

Walley was decked out in a fancy gray trench coat that complemented a handsome, clever face that was fighting to break free from a backwoods family. Sharp black hair and deep green eyes filled with more street sense than book smarts carried Walley's appearance into the form of a strikingly handsome leading man—but no matter what, no matter how many desperate measures Walley took, he still sounded like a backwoods hillbilly.

"I set a line across the road about five miles down," Walley explained. "The line is connected to the phone line. If the line is crossed, a low current is sent through the line and will cause the phone to let out a low buzz. Clever, huh?"

Brad had to admit that he was impressed. "I guess that college education you got in the navy paid off."

Walley didn't have time for his younger brother to puff him up. Brad was pushing thirty. His life was passing by, and it was time to grab some gold and live the good life. "Get outside and stay in the woods. When Sheriff Murphy shows up, plug him real good."

"Hey, wait a minute," Brad objected as Walley opened the front door. "Walley, I ain't killing Sheriff Murphy. I ain't no killer. You're the one who killed Patrick Brakemyer, not me. I ain't no killer."

"Listen here, boy!" Walley grabbed his brother by the throat. "You better do what I say, or I might kill you myself, do you hear me? I ain't—I'm not—in the mood for back talk. I brought you on board because I want you to live the good life with me, but if you go against me...*do* you want to go against me?" He narrowed his pair of vicious eyes and glared into Brad's scared eyes. "Do you?"

"No, Walley, you know I'm grateful to you...but I ain't got the guts to kill no man. Even if I wanted to plug Sheriff Murphy I couldn't...I ain't got the guts. You'd have to shoot me to make me pull the trigger—just ain't got the guts for it, you know that. When we were kids, I couldn't even shoot a deer. Just never had the guts. Remember how our old man used to always call me a no-good coward?"

"Yeah, and our man wasn't too far off in his speaking, either!" Walley shoved Brad against the front door and let go of his throat. "I'll have to kill Sheriff Murphy myself. Stay in the house."

"Uh, Walley," Brad pleaded, rubbing his throat. "Maybe you shouldn't kill Sheriff Murphy? I mean, look, we can just kill the lights that are on and lock the doors. Sheriff Murphy is probably doing one of those welfare checks—"

"Maybe our guests upstairs figured out a way to contact Sheriff Murphy? You ever think about that?" Walley hissed. "I didn't cut the main phone line, stupid. I only cut the lines to the phone downstairs and took all the phones upstairs away."

"Did you see anyone else other than Sheriff Murphy?" Brad asked.

"No, but—"

"Well, it would make sense in my head that if those people upstairs got a word out, Sheriff Murphy would charge up to this house with some reinforcement. I mean, that's how my mind sees it, Walley. I don't mean no disrespect and all." Brad glanced down. A cheap hunting rifle was leaning in the foyer's corner.

Walley stared into his brother's eyes, and then lifted his left hand and rubbed a sharp chin. "You know, Brad, you aren't so stupid sometimes. You just made a good valid point." Walley quickly considered his options. "Look, Brad, Tracy and her new...fella...think they're in control. They think they hired two stupid hillbillies they can write off when this is all over. They've got another thing coming, trust me, but right now we have to worry about Sheriff Murphy. If we can't kill him, then maybe we can wait him out? Maybe Sheriff Murphy will leave? If he doesn't..." he reached into his trench coat and pulled a hostile Glock 17 from a hidden shoulder holster. "I'll plug Sheriff Murphy myself."

"Yeah, okay, but Walley, don't you think this is going too far? I mean, we agreed to bring Patrick Brakemyer up here and hold him until Tracy Bates arrived. I didn't know you were going to kill—"

"Look!" Walley snapped, "Tracy Bates thinks Patrick Brakemyer is still alive. She doesn't know I forced the guy to give me the goods on her new fella. I've got everything under control, do you hear me, boy?"

"Yeah, Walley, but, did you have to kill him? I mean, he gave you the goods—"

"No one is leaving this mountain alive, is that clear?" Walley told his brother in a tone that caused Brad's blood to turn cold. "I've got everything under control." He glanced over his shoulder toward the staircase. "Mr. Private Eye is dead, but he gave me the goods. Kid thought he was smarter than me. But was he? No. No one is smarter than Walley Griffin." He continued to eye the staircase. "I don't know how Tracy Bates did it, but she found out that the mother of Bethany Lights is stashing millions in cash up here. Bethany Lights is going to tell us where the money is." He threw his head back at his brother. "If you had killed Davy Gray instead of being a yellow-belly coward, we would have only two scared women upstairs! Remind me to skin you alive and make you regret your choice later."

"But you said maybe I did right by letting Davy Gray live because you can use him against Tracy," Brad said shakily.

"Maybe I did, and maybe I'm right? We'll wait and see. In the meantime, get all the lights out and stay out of sight. I'll be outside."

"Don't kill Sheriff Murphy, Walley, I'm begging you. Killing a law man won't be right. Besides, if Sheriff Murphy doesn't show back up in town, that'll mean more law men will come up this way," Brad pleaded.

Walley's arrogant mind had not considered that fact. If he killed Sheriff Murphy, the man's death would only draw more vultures wearing badges. Walley despised it when his brother pointed out intelligent facts that he failed to recognize.

"Alright, boy. Just stay out of sight. I'll be outside watching Sheriff Murphy. If he gets too close, I'll plug him. Let's hope for his own good that he goes away." With those words, Walley snatched open the front door and stepped out into a frigid night. "Get the lights off and stay out of sight!" he snapped to Brad, and then vanished into an icy darkness.

Brad rapidly locked the front door. "Yeah, go play cowboy.

You're the one that's going to end up six feet under. I ain't got the guts to kill, but I'm sure gonna find the guts to kill you." He snatched up his hunting rifle. "I've got a bullet with your name on it, Walley…no, wait." A strange and sudden idea struck Brad's limited mind. "Maybe I'll let Sheriff Murphy deal with you!"

Without wasting a second, Brad darted upstairs. "You—in the bedroom!" he yelled once he reached the top of the stairs. "Come on out…I ain't gonna hurt you. I swear. You got my word!"

Bethany, Julie, and Davy all tensed up. "What do you want?" Davy yelled.

"Sheriff Murphy is on his way up the mountain road. My brother went outside to kill him…hell, maybe he will and maybe he won't!" He ran down the hallway that led to the bedroom Bethany and her friends were trapped in like a dumb bull. No matter. Brad had a plan, and his dismal mind had to act while the time to act was good.

He slid to a stop in front of a locked bedroom door. "Listen to me, now!" he yelled. "We ain't got time to be arguing with each other. We can either help each other or die —your choice. You better be smart about this because we ain't got a whole lot of time!"

Bethany looked at Julie and at Davy. "What have we got to lose? We heard the front door open and close, and we did hear some shouting take place downstairs."

"I agree with Bethany." Deep within her heart, Julie felt the need to support Bethany. Why? Julie sensed Bethany was the type of woman who possessed a rational mind and thought matters thoroughly through before acting. In her past, Julie had known friends who depended on knee-jerk reactions that resulted in catastrophic consequences. It was rare to find a friend who relied on patient, critical thinking skills.

"You best think fast because we might not have much time!" Brad yelled.

Davy took in the tone of Brad's voice. The man sounded anxious and downright urgent. "Bethany, I think you're right."

"Alright," Bethany lowered her voice to a whisper. "Davy, open the door. I'll go out first and Julie will follow. You step out right behind Julie and keep the gun behind your back. Stay behind Julie to hide most of your body. If you see the man out in the hallway try to harm anyone, shoot as fast as you can."

Davy was impressed. Bethany was a quick-thinking woman who clearly understood offensive strategies. "If we live through this, remind me to check your background and make sure you're not working for the CIA," he joked, and then drew in a deep breath. "Ready?"

Bethany and Julie nodded their heads.

"Okay, we're coming out...stand back."

Brad took a step back to wait and glare down the dark hallway. Only the light coming from the main hall hinted at any life in the area. He watched the bedroom door his prisoners were standing behind, and then tensed up when the door slowly opened. Bethany carefully stepped through the door, Julie quickly followed, and Davy took up the rear, staying behind Julie just enough to make it difficult for Brad to see his entire body.

Brad waved his left hand at everyone. "Come here, hurry, we ain't got much time."

Bethany glanced over her shoulder and focused back on Brad. He was holding a hunting rifle in his right hand in a nonthreatening tone. "Careful," she whispered to her friends, and then began easing forward up the hallway. "What do you want?" she asked Brad.

Davy peeked over Julie's shoulder. He spotted Brad holding his hunting rifle in a position that was extremely weak and vulnerable. It was clear the guy wasn't interested in harming anyone, but Davy wasn't about to take any chances.

He used his left hand to thrust Julie to the side and charged past Bethany, raising the gun he was holding into a clear firing position.

"Drop the rifle! Put it down now!"

Bethany and Julie froze in their tracks as Davy bravely raced forward. For a mere second, Bethany feared a bloody shoot-out might take place. But to her shock, Brad didn't freak out and try to shoot Davy. Brad didn't even pay any attention to Davy's threat. "Stop acting stupid, man. I told you I ain't here to kill you. My brother is the dangerous one. Now everyone, get up here!" Brad waved his left hand at Bethany and Julie again. "Hurry!"

Davy stopped about six feet from Brad, keeping a clear aim at the guy's chest. Bethany and Julie glanced at each other and rushed forward.

"What do you want?" Bethany asked Brad nervously, squinting at the bright light controlling the main hallway.

"Look, it's like this," Brad began hurriedly, glancing over his shoulder. "There's a whole lot of rats chewing on the same cheese. My brother is one of those rats, and he intends to kill everyone...including me. Sheriff Murphy is on his way up the mountain. My brother went outside to watch him when he arrives. Not sure if he's gonna plug Sheriff Murphy or not. Told him not to, I ain't no killer...I didn't kill that fella in the bedroom, either—my brother did." Brad looked back at everyone with anxious eyes. "Look, my brother threatened to kill me if I turned on him. If he knew I was talking to you, I'd be a dead man right now—"

Before Brad could finish speaking, a single bullet lashed up the stairs and struck Brad between his shoulder blades. Brad's body lurched forward, and then crumbled down onto the hallway floor, mere inches from Davy's feet.

"Down!" Davy yelled.

Bethany and Julie hit the hallway floor. As they did, Walley Griffin slammed the front door closed and made a clean escape into a—yes—dark and stormy night, leaving his brother lying dead inside of an old Victorian house.

Bethany heard the front door slam closed. "I think the shooter went out the front door!"

Davy crawled forward a few inches and checked on Brad, who was lying on the floor dead silent. The bullet Walley had fired had entered Brad's heart, causing instant death.

"I think he's dead. I can't get a pulse."

Bethany moved forward toward Davy and checked Brad's neck for a pulse. "No pulse in the neck...he's dead."

"Stay here. I'm going to check the downstairs!" Davy stayed low, crawling to the head of the stairs, and looking down. He didn't spot a single soul. "Looks clear. I'm going down."

Bethany grabbed Brad's hunting rifle. "Let's go, Julie. We're a team."

Julie tried not to look at Brad's dead body but failed. She spotted a lifeless face lying sideways on the hallway floor.

"How quick life is snuffed out. That could have been any of us, Bethany, at any second. Here, and then gone."

"I know, honey...trust me, I know." Bethany dared to stand up. She lowered her hand to help Julie stand. "Davy, I think the killer fled. If Sheriff Murphy is really on his way to the house, all we can do is wait."

"Let's go check the downstairs." Davy eyed the bottom of the stairs and began a downward passage on cautious legs.

Bethany and Julie followed. Bethany felt that any immediate threats had departed from the house—yet she felt that the man who killed Brad wasn't finished by a long shot. A high body count was still on the agenda.

chapter nine

Riley took a knee and checked Brad Griffin's body for a pulse. Brad was deader than a doornail. "And you say there's another dead man in the bedroom?" he asked gruffly.

Bethany nodded. "Yes."

Riley raised his eyes. Julie and Davy were looking down at him. "Any idea what's going on, Davy?" he asked.

Davy shook his head. "All this happened mighty fast, Riley. I dropped these ladies off and headed back down the mountain. Next thing I know, someone is shooting the tires out of my cab. After that, I ran back to this house. It's been a maze of thoughts ever since."

"Yeah. I found your cab on the side of the road." Riley stood up. "Didn't see any other vehicles. Thought I heard a four-wheeler chase off when I pulled up, but I couldn't be sure." Riley looked into Bethany's face. "Your mother told me she had a daughter who lived in Alaska."

"That's me." Bethany didn't recognize Riley. Riley seemed like a gruff, hard man in her eyes—a man she wanted to stand clear of. "My friend and I are taking a vacation—"

"A holiday," Julie cut in a quick, clean motion that gently bumped Bethany off to the side. "It's freezing in Alaska right now. Lots of snow, you know? When Bethany told me about the lovely lake house and suggested we take a holiday, I couldn't pass over the offer. It's hard eating frozen muffins and drinking lukewarm tea all winter."

"Uh-huh," Riley nodded without showing much interest. "Well, I better go look in the bedroom. Davy, take Ms. Lights and Ms. Walsh downstairs, make them some hot tea or something."

"Sure thing, Riley."

Bethany watched Riley walk off as if he didn't have a care in the world. *The death of that man doesn't bother him at all. He's as cold as ice.* Bitterness tapped Bethany's heart. *Oh, why get upset? We live in a hateful world full of hateful people.*

"Davy, I'll need to get in touch with my mother. I'm canceling the trip. Julie and I are...well, I don't know where we're going. Anywhere but here would be a good start, that's for certain."

"We'll ride back down the mountain with Riley," Davy informed Bethany, relieved that his two new friends had no desire to stay up on the mountain. "I'll come back up tomorrow with my brother and get the cab."

"Good." Bethany looked at Julie. "Want some coffee?"

"I could use a bite of solid food, to be perfectly honest," Julie admitted. "My tummy is a bit rumbly."

"Mine, too," Bethany confessed. "Mother said she stocked the kitchen for us."

"I stocked the kitchen," Davy admitted. "Yesterday, to be exact. There's food in the kitchen. Some good lunch meat in the refrigerator. Maybe some sandwiches might do the trick?"

"Sound good to me." Julie reached out and patted Bethany's hand. "Let's go eat, love, and then leave. I saw a hotel in town. We can stay there for tonight, and tomorrow we can rent a car and drive...anywhere but here. I think we'll be much safer on the open road."

"I think so, too. We still don't know who called and threatened you, and it's clear that this incident doesn't involve you personally." Bethany glanced around and sighed. "We were trapped in a very sudden and deadly situation and did our best to think our way through it. I'm not sure who the two dead men are or who the shooter was. It seems to me that the dead man lying in this hallway was shot dead before he could tell us the truth...shot dead by his own brother, I suppose. Well, no matter. Let's go, Julie."

Julie nodded and followed Bethany back down to the first floor. Davy followed carrying an old gun that no longer seemed important. The dangers of the night seemed to have passed. The house seemed at rest again—exhausted, but at rest. Davy didn't feel that an unknown killer would return to the house with Riley present. No. The killer had silenced a stool pigeon and fled into the storm. For now, Davy felt it was safe to have a sandwich with Bethany and Julie, and then travel back down the mountain. And that's exactly what he did.

While Bethany, Julie, and Davy got some solid food down, Riley checked the scene with trained eyes. He was a pilot accustomed to scanning the horizon for any unknown elements. Being a cop differed greatly from being a pilot, but the mechanisms of operation were still pretty much the same. Every operation had a system of order and protocols that had to be followed. A pilot always carried out a pre-flight checklist. A cop investigated a crime scene using a checklist. Yes, every operation had a system of order and protocols that worked. But as Riley checked the dead body of Patrick Brakemyer, he wasn't confident that following a strict order of operation was going to be the key to finding a deadly killer.

"I have a bad feeling you're the missing newlywed," he grunted under his breath as a bad feeling twisted the lower part of his gut. "Two dead men..."

Riley didn't recognize Brad Griffin. Why would he? Brad had lived and worked in Raleigh. Sure, Brad had grown up in Pine Lakes until he'd ditched high school, but after that, Pine

Lakes was left in his rear-view mirror. "Two dead men...an old house...two strange women...a friend who got stabbed in the back by a poisonous woman...and somehow, all of this is supposed to make sense." He shook his head and walked out of the bedroom on frustrated legs. Instead of going down to the kitchen, he walked back outside to his car and got Donald on the horn.

"Listen, son, we've got two dead men and a missing killer. Get Tom up here."

"Tom Stewart...county coroner...got it...two dead men...a killer..." Donald wrote down Riley's instructions as fast as he could, feeling as if the entire sky were falling on his head. His hand shook so badly as he wrote that each word ended up looking like a flattened coyote.

"Calm down, son," Riley ordered. "Call Edward and Victor. Wake them up and tell them I want them up here before they can wipe the sleep out of their eyes."

"Wake up two sleepy cops...got it..." Donald scribbled down two names he knew by heart. "Want me to come up—"

"You stay at the station, son," Riley said firmly. "The station has to be manned at all times. Communication is the key."

Donald nodded. "I'm the communication man. You can count on me!"

Riley rolled his eyes as hard ice struck the roof of his Oldsmobile. "I'm going back in the house. I'll be out of communication for a bit. I'll check back in with you in half an hour."

"I'll be here...call the coroner...two dead bodies...wake up two sleepy cops...I got everything!" Donald announced.

"Good. Sheriff out." Riley let out a heavy sigh, sat still for a moment, listened to the heavy storm batter his car, and dragged himself back inside a defeated house. He worked his way into a large kitchen that walked him back to the year 1894. For a minute, Riley felt that if he closed his eyes, he could walk back through time. "My deputy is getting the coroner on the move," he spoke in a voice that held little emotion. "Two more of my deputies will travel up the mountain in the next half hour or so."

Bethany and Julie were sitting at a vintage wooden table covered with a soft green tablecloth embroidered with little flowers. A plate of turkey sandwiches was sitting on the table along with a hot carafe full of hot coffee.

"Sandwich, Riley?" Davy asked. He was standing near a locked back door, holding a brown coffee cup in his right hand.

Riley had to admit that he was a bit hungry. A cup of hot coffee didn't sound so bad, either. "Might as well. We're not going anywhere anytime soon. It'll be daylight before we get back down the mountain." He searched for a spare coffee cup.

"Coffee cups are in that cupboard." Bethany pointed to a closed cupboard with a quick hand.

Riley nodded, found himself a clean coffee cup, and fetched himself a sandwich. "Mind pouring me some coffee?" he asked Bethany.

Bethany picked up the coffee carafe sitting in the middle of the kitchen table, filled Riley's coffee cup, and then set the carafe back down. "I suppose you want to ask us some questions?"

"In a second." To Bethany's shock, Riley bowed his head and prayed over the sandwich and coffee he was holding. "Lord, it's a tough night. Thank you for the provisions that will help. Your mercy is always present. In Jesus' sweet name I pray, amen."

"Amen," Bethany added.

Riley raised his head, took a bite of a delicious turkey sandwich, and sat down. "Your mother called the station and asked me to conduct a welfare check. She said she couldn't get through to you."

"Phone line was cut," Bethany explained. She returned to

her sandwich. *I didn't even consider that mother would try to call me. Of course, Mother would call to make sure Julie and I arrived safely and had everything we needed. Score one for the Lights family.*

"Well, it's a good thing your mother insisted I drive up here," Riley said flatly. He took another bite of his sandwich and continued. "My deputy got on the horn with me while I was driving up. A woman named Wanda Brakemyer called the station and reported her husband missing. According to my deputy, this Wanda Brakemyer sounded like she was in her twenties. I think the fella up in the bedroom might be the woman's missing husband. I'll have to get a positive identification, but the stiff isn't likely to be anyone else."

"That 'stiff' was once a living person, Sheriff Murphy," Bethany said acidly.

"Not anymore," Riley fired back in a tone that made Bethany bite down on her tongue. "Davy, you sure you don't know what's going on?"

"Wish I did," Davy confessed. He took a sip of coffee and focused his eyes on the back door. "My mind is chasing a lot of question marks right now."

Riley focused back on Bethany and Julie. "Ladies, I need you to tell me everything that you know."

Julie took a bite of her sandwich, chewed thoughtfully for a minute, and drank some coffee. "Sheriff Murphy, a man called and threatened me while I was in Alaska. My friend Bethany"—Julie nodded toward Bethany—"became worried and brought me to this mountain hoping that I would be safe."

"What man?" Riley asked.

"I don't know," Julie offered honestly. "All I do know—and this is a fact—the man who threatened me is not involved in what happened her."

"How do you know that?" Riley pressed.

"Riley, we heard the killer's voice. And the dead body

lying in the hallway, he talked to us. Both guys had a thick North Carolinian Mountain accent. Locals. Only I've never seen them before," Davy said without taking his eyes off the back door.

Riley looked toward Davy. "What bone are you chewing on, Davy? Why are you staring at the back door like that?"

"This." Davy nodded at the back door. "The doorknob, to be exact." Riley stood up and walked to the back door. Davy pointed at the doorknob.

"See that speck of pink?"

Riley leaned forward and spotted what appeared to be a little dust of pink stained on the doorknob.

"My ex-wife wears nothing but pink nail polish."

Bethany glanced at Julie. All Julie could do was take a bite of food and wait. "Davy—"

"Riley, Rachel Lights hired me to install generators in this house, to make sure this house had plenty of firewood, to stock this house full of food, and then to act as a personal chauffeur for her daughter for the next two weeks. Before you ask, I picked Mrs. Lights up from the airport and we got to talking. I told her I was an electrician. She asked a few personal questions, found out that I was living in my brother's garage apartment, one thing led to the next, and before I knew it, I had myself a side job." Davy nodded at the doorknob again. "I've been in this house more times in the last year than I can count. Initially, Mrs. Lights wanted the built-in generators for herself. I brought her wood and food, checked on her. When she called me and told me that her daughter was coming to visit, I was rehired."

"When was the last time Mrs. Lights was here?" Riley asked.

"Mrs. Lights visits every year on the anniversary of her husband's death," Davy explained. "She used to hire Timmy Logan to help her, but Timmy died last year of cancer." He continued to stare at the back doorknob. "That pink paint wasn't on that doorknob when I last left this kitchen. The color pink always draws my eyes to it. Tracy is a pink addict."

"Davy, I can dust for prints and see what I come up with. Other than that, I can't arrest a woman because you found some pink nail polish on a doorknob."

"No, but maybe you can have one of your deputies drive over to the house that woman stole from me and see if she's home?" Davy suggested, bitterness twisting his voice.

"Yeah, I can do that." Riley bent down and touched the speck of pink paint that was staining a brass doorknob. "I was at the school board meeting when Tracy Gray—I mean, Tracy Bates—got the boot. I noticed all the pink the woman was wearing, too. But it's like I said, I can't go arrest a woman for wearing pink."

"Yeah. Too bad," Davy let out a tired grunt and then finally turned away from the back door. "Bethany, Julie, if my ex-wife is behind this mess, I'm truly sorry. I would never endanger your lives."

"We know that, Davy," Bethany assured her friend. *Pink nail polish on the back door. Mother hates pink. Who else could it be other than Davy's ex-wife? The only problem is, I don't have a clue about this awful night. There are too many broken pieces of glass to pick up.* She took a slow sip of coffee and then focused on getting a solid bite of food down. What else could she do?

Outside in the storm, Walley Griffin made his way down a back trail on a speeding four-wheeler. He was far from finished with murder.

chapter ten

Cold, dark-gray skies pregnant with snow roamed over the Pine Lakes Inn. By noon, a fresh foot of snow had dropped onto the little town. School had been happily canceled—again. Most businesses closed—again. People of all ages were out enjoying the snow—sledding, skiing, building snowmen or snow forts, or just out taking a cold walk. Not a single citizen had a clue that two murders had taken place up on Old Wolf Mountain at the old Lights lake house. Riley had ordered his people to zip their lips or else, and no one dared ruffle Riley's feathers. Bethany had no desire to ever see Riley again, let alone anger the man. She was content sitting in a nice, warm hotel room with Julie, sipping on a cup of hot coffee.

"Davy will be by tomorrow to pick us up. He'll drive us to Raleigh. We'll rent a car there and drive west."

Julie watched Bethany take a sip of coffee from a lousy paper cup that came with the hotel room. Bethany looked a little tense. "Your mother was really upset, wasn't she, love?"

Bethany set her coffee cup down onto a round table and folded her arms over her dark green sweater. "Yes. Mother was very upset. She has forbidden me to ever go near the lake house again. She is considering putting the lake house and the mountain land up for sale."

"Oh, what a pity." Julie sat down on the edge of a soft queen-sized bed with a sigh. "I hope your mother will not take such drastic actions."

Bethany watched her friend scan a heavy brown winter jacket that was a bit too large. The jacket in question had once been hanging on a rack inside O'Malley's Department Store in Snow Falls. Amanda adored it, though Sarah wasn't as enthusiastic. Without Amanda knowing, Sarah had marked the jacket ninety percent off. Julie had happily bought it—a jacket that had sat unsold for over three years. Sarah told Amanda that a happy shopper had finally bought the lovely jacket. Amanda accepted the...truth and forgot all about the matter until she saw her cousin wearing it. When Julie told Amanda how she had found the jacket marked at ninety percent off...well, let's just say that Amanda ate all the kosher chili dogs at O'Mally's Department Store on purpose just to annoy Sarah. Revenge was sweet.

"I doubt Mother will get rid of the lake house and the land. Family value bears more weight than fear."

"Yes, let's hope so." Julie considered putting down another cup of coffee, but the idea of drinking such horrid coffee made her stomach cringe. "Want to walk down to the diner? It's a little past lunch time."

"Is it?" Bethany checked her wristwatch. "My goodness, it seems like we just woke up." Bethany looked at two queen-sized beds sitting side by side. The idea of rooming alone after experiencing a deadly night up on Old Wolf Mountain hadn't appealed to Bethany or Julie. The two friends decided that staying in the same room might be safer—or more comforting—than rooming alone. "We've been at this hotel for two days now, and it seems like we just left the mountain."

"At least the killer hasn't showed up," Julie pointed out.

Bethany took a slow sip of coffee. "Davy's ex-wife is out of town, too. She hasn't shown up. According to Davy's neighbor, Tracy Bates left to visit New York the day before we arrived. Good timing, I would say."

Julie stood up and walked over to a long window covered with a thick brown curtain. She eased part of the curtain back and peered out into a white winter wonderland. "It's snowing heavily, love. The weather is forecasting more snow for the next three days. It's so lovely outside, picturesque. It's such a shame to leave. The lake house would be so lovely to be at right now."

"I know. I was looking forward to staying at the lake house—" Bethany suddenly stopped.

Julie spun around. "What is it, love? Did you spill some hot coffee on you?"

"No, I..." *What?* Bethany asked herself. *Could it be that the killer returned to the lake house? No one is there right now. No one is at the lake house. Sheriff Riley marked the lake house off-limits. Tracy Bates is out of town…*

"Uh oh. I know that look. You're having an idea," Julie winced.

"No, no...I'm just wondering where the killer went to. Sheriff Riley said he heard what sounded like a four-wheeler speeding off when he arrived. Did the killer drive down the mountain and escape? We know that the man he shot is Brad Griffin. We know that the other man—the dead man we found in the bedroom—is Patrick Brakemyer. And according to Sheriff Murphy, Walley Griffin, Brad Griffin's brother, died last year in a car accident. Yet, Brad Griffin insisted his brother was the killer. Brad Griffin's records show that he doesn't have any other siblings."

"Love, we talked about this. It's a mystery, I agree, but I don't really feel confident in entertaining the idea of opening back up a case that needs to be closed." Julie hated to throw cold water onto Bethany's face, but her heart wasn't enthusiastic about diving back into a dark pool filled with murder. Julie still had no idea who had called and threatened her.

"I know, but my mind keeps thinking about all this, Julie. Maybe it's the writer in me? Maybe I'm just hungry for punishment? Maybe I'm insane? Who knows?" Bethany stood up, rubbed the back of her neck, and joined Julie at the window. "I just keep getting the feeling that this isn't over— for Davy, at least. I keep feeling that Davy's life is in danger."

Julie studied Bethany's eyes, and then looked out at the snow. Whether she wanted to entertain the idea of learning how to swim in a pool of murder or not, the one thing Julie couldn't do was leave a friend to drown.

"Okay, love. I'm all ears."

Bethany reached out her hand and patted Julie's shoulder. "You poor woman. You've become best friends with the wrong person, haven't you? You relocated to Snow Falls hoping to find peace, and instead got tangled up with me."

Julie forced a strained smile to her face. "I can deal with you, love. You're like a sister to me now. What I can't deal with is all the killings I've seen. Murder is hideous, and cruel."

"That's true, but there are good people in this world. Remember Pete, Sarah's friend who lives in Los Angeles?"

A tender smile replaced Julie's frown. "Pete is very wonderful. He's a gem."

"I wholeheartedly agree," Bethany nodded. "And what about Sarah and Amanda. And Conrad? What about Andrew? Everyone back in Snow Falls?"

"My cousin Amanda is a nut," Julie said, laughing a little. "Amanda could clean out ten buffets without blinking an eye. Poor Sarah can't keep any kosher hotdogs stocked in the snack cafe at O'Mally's. Plus, Amanda cheats when she plays Scrabble with Conrad. I can't prove it, but I know that cousin of mine cheats."

Bethany grinned. When Amanda and Conrad played a game of Scrabble, a dangerous war began. Everyone ducked low and took cover. "Our friends are a little curious, aren't they?" Bethany asked. "I suppose I should have told Sarah that you received a threatening phone call. Maybe it was wrong of me to run off with you the way I did. I just—and this may sound a tad egotistical—I just don't want Sarah thinking I can't take care of myself, or you. It's so important to me to make everyone believe I can handle every snowball that is thrown at me. Including you, honey."

Julie turned her eyes back to Bethany and saw a heavy frown appear on her friend's face.

"Love, you don't have anything to prove to me or anyone else. You're loved just for who you are. But I see you strive so hard to present yourself as a powerful woman. Why? Because deep down, you're scared...just like me. We've both embarked on a new life, we're struggling to leave a painful past behind, and we have no idea what the future truly holds for us. If we lose grip on our ability to maintain what control we do have on our lives...who knows, love? We might stumble and fall down a deep hole."

"I suppose crawling out of a hideous hole filled with years of pain will take time," Bethany sighed.

"Healing takes time, love." Julie patted Bethany's arm. "Remember how pretty and cozy O'Mally's was last Christmas?" Bethany nodded. "Snow Falls is such a lovely little Alaskan town, and O'Mally's is a wonderful addition. The store is ancient and vintage, and Sarah and Amanda do such a wonderful job keeping the store up and making it feel like a winter wonderland inside. Last Christmas, even though murder tainted the air, was very beautiful. Through the ugliness, I kept thinking to myself that when the gray clouds pass, a beautiful rainbow will appear over Snow Falls. I still have that hope, love. I still want to see another Christmas in Snow Falls. I still want to visit O'Mally's and watch Sarah fuss at Cousin Amanda for eating all the kosher chili dogs, and maybe find me another jacket." Julie tugged on the jacket she was wearing. "A coat as ugly as the one I'm wearing," she laughed.

Bethany smiled. "Well, your coat is—"

"Ugly, but I love it," Julie laughed again and nudged Bethany with her shoulder. "We're going to be okay, you and me, wait and see. Right now, we're...well, we're finding our legs, as you Americans sometimes say. We're not going to blossom overnight, you know? We're two works of art in progress."

"More like two cold slices of pizza that need to be warmed up," Bethany smiled. "We're not exactly young chickens anymore, Julie. We're two women who are in their forties."

"Well, someday, when we turn fifty, we'll be two bowls of cold soup that need warmed up." Julie nudged Bethany with her shoulder again. "Now, how about we walk down to the diner and get some lunch? I'm hungry, and this hotel coffee is making me want to gag. I want a fresh cup of hot coffee that tastes like coffee instead of mud."

"Okay, honey. I could use a bite to eat—"

A hard hand knocked on the hotel room door.

"It's Davy. You girls in there?"

"We're here! Just a second, Davy." Bethany hurried to the room door, disengaged a secure lock, and peeled the door open. Davy appeared wearing a heavy brown coat and a brown muffler hat soaked with snow. "I wasn't expecting to see you until—"

"We need to talk," Davy spoke urgently. "I...it's not proper for a man to enter a woman's hotel room. Call me old-fashioned, but that's how I am. I was raised on the Bible. Meet me at the diner in twenty minutes." Davy threw a pair of alert eyes around the snow. "I don't think I'm being watched…but be careful walking to the diner."

"Davy, what's this all about?" Bethany demanded.

"Tracy." Davy lowered his voice, barely speaking over an icy, howling wind. "Tracy called me. I'll explain at the diner. Just be careful. I don't think Walley Griffin is dead." Before Bethany could ask any more questions, Davy turned and walked away.

Bethany stuck her head out of the door, but didn't see Davy's cab parked anywhere. She watched Davy walk away on foot, trudging through deep snow.

"Love?" Julie asked, sticking her head out of the door, and looking around.

Bethany bit down on her lower lip and scanned a white, frozen land for a few minutes. As far as she could tell, no one was in sight. The back of the hotel faced a cozy river. Beyond the river was nothing but a white forest. Bethany didn't spot anybody hiding beyond the river.

"Let's get our coats on, Julie. I have a bad feeling that Davy is in trouble."

"Does this mean we're not leaving, tomorrow, love?" Julie winced.

"I'm afraid so," Bethany confessed, and then let out a miserable groan. "We're going to have to stay in Pine Lakes a few more days."

Walley Griffin didn't hear Bethany speak to Julie. He was back at the lake house hiding out...waiting for Tracy Bates to arrive.

"I've got everyone where I want them. All I must do is put all the pawns back on the chess board and finish the game. No one outsmarts Walley Griffin! No one! I'm going to kill them all and get the money!"

chapter eleven

The smell of syrupy pancakes, fried eggs, sizzling sausage, and hot coffee filled the interior of a delightful diner that reminded Bethany of a gingerbread house. The Pine Lakes Diner was older than time but was still owned by the original family—a family that worked diligently to maintain a strong, family atmosphere based on Biblical values. Red-nosed children were huddled in warm booths next to smiling parents. Old men were sitting along the front counter drinking coffee and jabbering away. A group of old women were nestled in a far back booth, talking about a church bake sale. Yes, the diner was a tender hometown heartbeat that comforted many people.

"My, the diner is crowded. We won't be able to get a booth," Julie told Bethany, standing behind a line of people who were putting down their names for a reservation.

"Not any time soon." Bethany bit her bottom lip and searched for Davy, who was nowhere in sight. "Where is Davy?" she asked Julie.

"I'm not sure. Should we go back outside?"

"I will." Bethany checked the diner once more. "Will you stay and make us a reservation?"

Julie nodded. "I don't mind standing in this warm, delightful air and smelling all the goodies that are cooking."

Bethany smiled, knowing Julie didn't mind her task at all. "I'll be outside looking for Davy. I won't go far."

"Stay within yelling distance, love," Julie begged.

Bethany nodded, adjusted a green and white wool scarf that she had wrapped around her neck, and ventured back outside into a hard falling snow tossed around by icy, howling winds. The front parking lot of the diner was stacked with snow, with not a single vehicle present. Everyone was walking to the diner. Why not? It was a fun snow day—and besides, only the main streets were plowed. The diner sat on a cozy side street facing a lazy river. *I don't see Davy. I see families walking about...a group of kids off in the distance throwing snowballs...over there is a young couple holding hands...there's a man on a pair of skis...but no Davy.*

A husband and wife walked up to the front of the diner with a pair of laughing kids trudging behind them. "How bad is it inside?" a short, plump man with a jolly face asked Bethany with a cheerful smile.

"Crowded, I'm afraid," Bethany responded, struggling to sound pleasant. Riley was doing a good job keeping his little community blind to fear. Bethany tossed her eyes at the two boys who appeared to be twins, and then glanced at a smiling woman who personified the perfect housewife. "You have a beautiful family."

"Well, only in public," the man laughed. "At home, we take off our masks."

"Oh, John." The woman playfully slapped her husband's arm with a heavy blue mitten. "My husband is only kidding."

"Can we go inside, Dad? Huh?" the twin boys begged.

"We better go inside and put our names down for a booth or we may never get a bite to eat," the man smiled. "It was nice meeting you," he told Bethany warmly, and then hurried his family into the cozy diner.

"Life must be so beautiful for some people. It seems like that married couple is so happy. I was married to a monster, but that lady seems to be married to a wonderful man." Bethany dropped her eyes and stared down at snow that almost came up to her knees. *I stayed married. I could have walked away from my marriage at any time. It's nobody's fault but my own. Yes, I was raised to remain committed to a marriage—to protect the family name, to always present an acceptable appearance in the public eye—but I could have walked away. I wasted so many good years of my life trying to love the wrong man. I became so bitter, I wrote a book about the perfect murder...and now look at me. Instead of settling down and enjoying the years I have ahead of me, I'm standing out here in the cold looking for a missing man. Am I cursed? Why can't I be that amiable woman who just went into the diner, holding the arm of a loving man with two beautiful children in tow?*

Bethany continued to stare down at the snow as a wave of self-pity began washing over her heart. Being a woman was tough business—not like smooth baking oil wrapped around a pie pan. Bethany guessed being a man wasn't easy, either. Being human, for that matter, was a battle; man or woman, it didn't matter. Life was hard for everyone at times. Still, Bethany allowed herself to dip into a pool of self-pity.

However, her time in the pool was quickly interrupted by a hard voice.

"Bethany Lights?"

"Huh?" Bethany raised her eyes. A tall, gruesome-looking man wearing a face that immediately reminded her of a filthy trash can appeared in the snow. Bethany's mind quickly scanned the man's appearance and clothes. *Tall...wearing a black trench coat...black ski hat...black pants...black boots...looks like a piece of slime you would find inside of a dirty trash can.*

"Are you Bethany Lights?" Ralph Polonzio asked in a thick Brooklyn accent.

"Who wants to know?"

Ralph stared at Bethany through eyes that appeared rotted to the core. "Here's the deal, lady," he spoke menacingly. "There's a dirty game being played. I'm the game master. If you want to live, you better listen to every word I say. Understand?"

Foul breath oozed from Ralph's mouth and splattered onto Bethany's face. Bethany had to lower her face and turn her head in order not to vomit. *This guy smells like rotted whiskey, day-old eggs and decayed trash.* "You must be the sleazy lawyer Tracy Bates snagged."

"Watch your mouth before I smack you good!" Ralph snapped.

Bethany threw her eyes forward in a daring manner. "Go ahead and try to smack me." She plowed into Ralph. "I've taken countless self-defense courses. I'll fight you with everything I have and more." Bethany pulled her right hand out of the coat she was wearing. Her daddy's old gun appeared in the snow. "Or maybe I'll shoot you?"

Ralph looked down at the gun Bethany was holding and peered up into a pair of eyes that would not hesitate to kill. "You got guts. I like that," he told Bethany. "My apologies for being so rough with my mouth." He glanced around. "To answer your question—no, I'm not the sleazy lawyer Tracy Bates snagged. My brother Tony, he's the sleazy lawyer. I'm just the guy who is controlling the game."

"What game?" Bethany put her gun away before anyone could see.

"Look," Ralph snarled, "it's like this: I want the money because maybe I got a lot of debts and Mr. Marizzo is breathing down my neck. Maybe Tracy Bates got bored in this little village and made a few trips to New York in the past, maybe she placed some foul bets that put her in debt? Maybe we were an item at one time, maybe I introduced her to my brother, the lawyer? Maybe my brother owes me a few favors? Maybe he wants to keep his brains in his skull?

Maybe Mr. Marizzo has it out for my brother? Maybe I talked Mr. Marizzo into sparing his miserable life? Maybe my brother is playing a sick game right now? Get it?"

"No," Bethany offered an honest answer. "I don't get all the maybes. All I get is that Davy Gray is missing."

"Yeah, Davy Gray is missing. Two guesses who took him?" Ralph darted his eyes around them. "My brother isn't stupid, lady. He isn't as smart as me, and I never even went to some fancy college. But he isn't stupid."

Two brothers again? Weren't Brad and Walley Griffin enough? Bethany drew in an icy breath of air.

"What do you want?" she asked.

Ralph nodded. "Walk with me."

Bethany glanced over her shoulder and looked at the warm, safe diner standing behind her. Was Julie watching the scene? Most likely.

"No. I'm staying where people can see me."

"I'm not going to whack you, lady," Ralph promised. "I've killed a rat or two in my past, but I've never hurt a woman. Maybe I smacked a smart-mouth once or twice, but hey, it's important to teach people manners."

"I'm sure it is." Bethany felt like slapping Ralph across his smart, arrogant mouth. "We stay close to the diner. We'll walk toward the river."

"Good enough." Ralph examined the scene, spotted families and children playing in the snow, and then nodded. "Let's walk."

Bethany drew in a brave breath and forced her legs to move. "What's this all about?"

"Your old lady has millions in cash hidden up at that fancy house on the mountain," Ralph spoke in a low, stern tone. "Maybe you know about the cash, and maybe you don't. But if you want to live, you're going to have your old lady tell me where the cash is."

Mother? Hiding millions in cash at the lake house? that's

insane. Mother barely carries ten dollars in cash in her change purse. What in the world is going on? I better play along until I get some solid answers.

"Alright. You want money. I can understand that. How does this all connect? How is Tracy Bates involved? How was Patrick Brakemyer involved? How was Brad Griffin involved?"

"Hey, do I look like I'm on *Jeopardy*, lady?" Ralph snapped. "I'm not a fountain of information."

"But you do have the answers I want," Bethany insisted.

Ralph glanced over into Bethany's stony face through a heavy falling snow. "Maybe I like your attitude, maybe I don't. We'll see, huh?"

"I want answers."

"Maybe you do." Ralph continued through the deep snow without missing a beat. "Look, maybe Tracy Bates wanted her husband dead, and maybe I was for hire at the time? Maybe Tracy's bookie called me and introduced me to Tracy?"

"Stop with the maybes. Speak clearly," Bethany demanded.

Ralph tossed a sour eye at Bethany. "Maybe Davy Gray had a nice life insurance policy, huh? But then, maybe at the last moment, the rat dropped his policy? Maybe he wasn't so dumb, huh?"

Davy doesn't strike me as a stupid man. "Maybe Davy had good reason to drop his life insurance policy." Bethany struggled through the snow until she drew near to a sleepy river and stopped. "This is as far as we go."

Ralph glanced around. No one was within earshot. Only the sound of a lazy flowing river could be heard over the icy winds.

"Look, Tracy Bates wanted her husband dead. She has debts, get it? When Davy dropped his life insurance policy, she hit the roof. Even if she divorced her husband, what would she get? Pennies?"

"A house, a business..."

"Pennies!" Ralph snapped. "So maybe that black widow came up with a plan?"

"What plan?" Bethany asked, ignoring the stinging winds striking her face.

"Divorce the rat she was married to, take him to the bank. Make it seem all legit and whatnot. And then kill him."

"Why kill Davy if he doesn't have a life insurance—" Bethany asked.

"Hey, zip your mouth and let me talk," Ralph snapped. "It isn't nice to interrupt all the time."

Bethany resisted the urge to roll her eyes. "My apologies."

"That's better." Ralph glanced around again. "Tracy wanted Davy dead because she convinced her bookie the rat still had a life insurance policy. About that time, Mr. Marizzo was thinking about killing my brother. Now, I don't like my brother, but hey, I also don't want my mother crying a river of tears on my shoulder. So I talked Mr. Marizzo into keeping my brother alive. Maybe Mr. Marizzo would erase some of my debts if I killed a man for him. Maybe I did, maybe I didn't?"

This rotted piece of trash is quite an act. "I'm all ears."

Ralph nodded. "Maybe Tracy still wanted me to kill Davy. Maybe that spider was playing a dangerous game that I found out about. You see, Tracy had her eyes on taking control of Pine Lakes—all of Pine Lakes. She had a friend on the school board who helped her become principal of some dumb little school. Maybe during that time Davy Gray was supposed to die? Maybe the guy's death was going to be blamed on his brother...and maybe the guy's brother is married to a woman who is just as dark-hearted? Maybe them two dames got a plan?"

chapter twelve

"Davy's brother's wife?"

"Hey, you heard me the first time!" Ralph spat at the snow. "Maybe Davy Gray's brother is married to a woman who became real friendly with your old lady? Maybe one day, your old lady accidentally forgot her pocketbook after a meeting and a pair of itchy hands stole a financial ledger out of the pocketbook before returning it? Maybe Tracy and her new friend created a plan?"

"I'm trying to keep up—"

"It's like this," Ralph growled." Tracy Bates is keeping a hungry bookie at bay until she can pay off her debt. If she can't, it's lights out for her. But Tracy isn't so stupid. Sure, she was in panic mode at first, but she calmed down after her friend told her about your old lady's...financial secrets. How do I know all this? I hired Patrick Brakemyer. The kid was my cousin's best friend and had a good head on his shoulders. Real smart, you know? Patrick did good in digging up the dirt for me."

"Can we pause for a minute?" Bethany asked. "I'm still not sure how your brother plays into this."

"Maybe I found out the truth and played a little game

myself after Patrick gave me the goods? So maybe I had Patrick do some digging on the judge that was going to be presiding over Tracy's divorce case? Maybe Patrick dug up some dirt on the guy? Maybe I spun a tale for my brother and forced him to represent Tracy, and maybe my brother liked Tracy...or maybe Tracy decided to play my brother? Everything became like quicksand when Tracy betrayed me, when my brother told her I had the goods on her."

Bethany shook her head. *Goodness, the more people involved, the more confused I become.*

"Okay, let me get this straight in my mind...Tracy Bates took trips to New York—"

"To get away from Mayberry, sure. Nothing wrong with that, huh?" Ralph asked.

"I guess not," Bethany answered, and shook her head again. "While in New York, she gained a high gambling debt."

"The woman liked the night life. Can't blame her." Ralph tugged on the collar of his trench coat. "Sometimes there's a back room full of fun. Sometimes a bookie hangs around in the shadows. That's the way of it."

"I'm sure it is." *This guy is surely a rotted piece of trash.* "Somehow you meet Tracy Bates."

"At a night club in Brooklyn. Meet lots of dames at the clubs."

"I'm sure you do." Bethany resisted the urge to shoot Ralph on the spot. "Tracy gets into trouble and what...comes to you for help?"

"Hey, I'm a knight in shining armor."

"No, you're not!" Bethany snapped. Ralph prepared to fire back, but Bethany took control. "You're a sleazy, back-alley piece of trash!"

"I told you to watch your mouth, lady!" Ralph raised his right hand. Bethany whipped out her daddy's old gun before he could blink an eye. He shook his head. "Too bad you're a smart mouth. We could be an item."

"Never." Bethany lowered the gun, looked around, and continued. "You two killed Davy Gray. Davy must have caught wind, dropped his life insurance policy to protect himself. But Tracy is still in trouble. She tells her bookie she's still going to kill her husband. Somewhere in between, a devious woman married to Davy's brother finds my mother's pocketbook...I'll have to work that out in my mind later." Bethany lowered her voice. "Tracy comes up with a plan, right? She needs you dead because you have the goods. So she romanced your brother, right?"

"Hey, you're smart. Too bad you have a smart mouth," Ralph growled.

Bethany ignored Ralph's rotted insult. She had to think fast, because Ralph wasn't standing in front of her because he was preparing to play nice. No way. Ralph had a deadly plan of his own that involved the deaths of two innocent women.

"Tracy Bates went to Mr. Marizzo, didn't she?" Bethany asked.

Ralph's eyes grew wide.

"Hey, how did you...I mean..." Ralph tripped over his words, and then tumbled down. "You're smart, lady," he sneered. "Maybe you're too smart? Maybe I underestimated you?"

"Two women can't take over an entire town alone," Bethany pointed out. "No. I'm thinking that Tracy Bates and your brother went to Mr. Marizzo...whoever that is...and complimented the man's ears with a bunch of hideous words."

Ralph glared at Bethany with eyes that glowed with raw anger. "Maybe my brother got Mr. Marizzo off his back and maybe he made me a marked target, huh? Maybe Mr. Marizzo runs drugs? Maybe Mr. Marizzo wants to get out of

New York? Maybe Mr. Marizzo agreed to pay off Tracy's debts and kill me instead? Maybe I'm not going to let that happen!" Ralph spat on the ground again. "Maybe I underestimated my brother. Maybe I went a little soft instead of letting Mr. Marizzo whack him."

"Maybe," Bethany nodded, slowly becoming accustomed to how Ralph talked. "So let me think...Davy and his brother had to die, right?"

"Kill Davy Gray because he knew too much. The guy may act stupid, but he's not," Ralph confirmed. "And then send his brother down the river for the murder."

"Is it really that simple?"

"No," Ralph confessed. "Tracy found out her ex-husband was working for your old lady. Now, call that a stroke of luck or mere coincidence—hey, you're smart, you draw your own conclusions. All I know is that things started going downhill for her after she got canned from her job as principal. Seems like folks in this village don't like bad morals. Tracy never could keep her beliefs to herself; she always ran her mouth off. Anyways, after Tracy was fired, maybe Mr. Marizzo started having second thoughts, huh?"

"So what happened?" Bethany asked.

"Tracy is convinced that your old lady is hiding millions in cold cash up at that mountain house," Ralph said, throwing his eyes around the snow. "When she found out that you and your friend were coming for a visit...well, things just kind of clicked in her mind. She saw a way to force your old lady to tell her where the money is hidden while killing off all her enemies in one swoop."

"How?" Bethany asked, even though she had an idea.

"Lady, you got brains. Think about it. Brad Griffin is dead. The guy wasn't a genius, you know? Tracy found herself two dumb toads to control. Walley Griffin met Tracy at a club in Raleigh...they talked, words were exchanged, that's how it works. My brother flew back to New York to talk with Mr. Marizzo when Tracy went to Raleigh. She's a patient spider, but her time is growing short and she knows that."

"Keep talking."

"Hey, don't push me!" Ralph narrowed his eyes. "Tracy decided it was time for everyone to die so she called me and spewed a bunch of lies while crying crocodile tears. She told me my brother was planning to kill her. She promised to share all the money with me if I killed my brother. A bunch of filth!" Ralph spat at the snow again. "She set my brother up with the same lie, and then called Mr. Marizzo and told him her plan and promised to give him all the money if he spared her life. Why? Because Mr. Marizzo paid off her debts and Tracy was now in debt to him. She begged Mr. Marizzo to come to the mountain house. Why?"

"She wanted to kill him."

"Bingo," Ralph nodded. "Patrick was recording every word Tracy spoke and giving the goods to me." He glanced around. "I played along with Tracy. My brother? Let's just say I'm not soft toward him. That rat told Tracy he would kill me for her, and he meant it. That rat is wrapped up in a deadly spider web...but no matter. He's a dead man." He paused, his eyes still shifting. "So it all came down to putting everyone in the same house at different times. First you and your friend show up, then Walley and his kid brother would snag you and kill Davy. Easy. Then I would show up. My brother would be waiting in the shadows and plug me with a bullet in the back of the head. Then Tracy would have Walley and his kid brother kill my brother. Okay, not so bad. Then Mr. Marizzo would show up, see the scene, and be satisfied...and then Tracy would have him force you to tell him where the money is. And trust me, lady, Mr. Marizzo has ways of making people talk."

"But I don't know where—"

"Let me finish!" Ralph snapped. "Maybe Tracy had Walley and his kid brother kill Mr. Marizzo and then kill off her friend, the dame who's married to Davy's brother? Don't forget about her."

"I haven't."

Ralph stared deeply into Bethany's eyes. "Maybe Patrick got too smart for his own good and came up with a few ideas himself, huh? Maybe the kid wanted to score a handful of cash for his pretty new wife? Maybe he got too big for his pants, huh? And maybe Walley Griffin plugged him real good? Maybe I was in the house the entire time and seen and heard everything? Maybe I was hiding good?"

"You were in the lake house."

"Lake house, mountain house, who cares?" Ralph snapped. "Yeah, I was in the house, lady. Tracy and my brother were in Raleigh. Davy's brother's wife—hey, maybe we got a thing for each other? Maybe she's been kind of giving me a few tips, too? Maybe Tracy believes her friend is loyal? Maybe the dame has her own plans?"

"Good grief, how many plans are there?" Bethany exclaimed.

"Lady, when it comes to money, your own mother will slit your throat," Ralph told Bethany in a voice that caused the woman's blood to turn colder than the icy winds attacking her face.

"I suppose."

"Maybe Mr. Marizzo got a call from me, huh?" Ralph asked. "Maybe I let him hear all the goods Patrick gave me? And maybe...just maybe...Mr. Marizzo is going to do me a favor and kill Tracy Bates...my brother...Walley Griffin...and yeah, even the dame who put a knife in her friend's back."

"Davy's brother's wife?"

"That's the dame," Ralph confirmed. "All it comes down to is the money. Tell me where the money is. If you don't know, force your old lady to tell you."

"If I don't?" Bethany asked.

"Look, I ain't one to hurt a lady, but I assure you…" Ralph bent his rotted eyes forward. "Mr. Marizzo knows you live in Alaska, lady. He knows where your old lady lives. He knows who all your relatives are. If you don't cooperate, he's going to make you suffer real bad. Ever see an old woman's head being squeezed by a vice grip? Ever see a pair of eyes pop out of someone's head? Maybe you don't want to see your old lady's eyes do that, huh?" Ralph asked, tossing a diseased grin at Bethany.

I should shoot this snake where he stands. "Davy—"

"My brother snagged Davy. The guy is probably dead by now." Ralph shrugged. "His brother has been snagged, too. Walley Griffin is playing a deadly game of lies…no matter, my brother is going to force Walley to kill Davy, film it, and then blackmail the rat to kill everyone else on his list. My brother isn't stupid; just stupid with women." He shook his head. "Tracy Bates is a looker…a real nice looker. Can't figure why she married a guy like Davy Gray, some small-town nobody. All Tracy ever did was complain about Mr. Goody-Two Shoes to me. Can't figure it out."

Or can you? Or better yet, can I? As confusing as this sounds, maybe, just maybe, Davy's brother and Tracy Bates have a plan? Maybe a bitter wife found out that her husband was going after Tracy Bates and came up with a plan on her own? Maybe all this boils down to Davy's brother's wife. I know there's a lot of other confusing question marks attached to different players in this game, but a very mysterious woman might have been playing Tracy Bates all along—and her husband—to extract revenge. I'm sure the process became difficult when Tracy started involving other players, but the basic theme remains the same: start at the beginning and work your way forward. That's how you find the answers that lead to hidden truths.

"I'll call my mother and talk to her. What's my time limit?"

"You're smart," Ralph told Bethany in a pleased tone.

"You have twenty-four hours. Mr. Marizzo will arrive in Pine Lakes tomorrow afternoon. If, by then, you want to play dumb...well, just remember, he likes to play with the vice grips and he don't care if he's playing with a man or a woman. Mr. Marizzo isn't soft like me." He glanced around. "I'll be in touch…no cops or else. Stay at the hotel, and hey, nice town you got here. I think I'm going to like it here."

With those parting words, Ralph strolled away like a snake slithering through the snow.

Bethany watched Ralph walk back to the diner, glance around, and vanish behind the right side of the diner. She wanted to follow the guy, but she spotted Julie bursting out of the diner and running toward her.

Bethany waved her hands to show Julie that she was alright and then waited beside the river.

"Bethany, who was that? Are you alright, love?" Julie asked breathlessly.

Bethany waited until Julie could catch her breath. The poor woman was breathing out white streams of smoke like a thundering locomotive.

"I'm alright," she promised. "The man—no, the piece of trash—I was speaking to was Ralph Polonzio, some sewer rat from New York." She scanned the snow to make sure she didn't see any suspicious eyes watching her. "Honey, Davy has been kidnapped."

"Kidnapped? Oh my goodness, we have to—"

"Julie, I think Davy let himself be taken, though I can't be sure." Bethany bit her lower lip as heavy flakes of snow dropped down onto her shoulders. "Julie, we have a lot of dangerous players fighting on the same field. But right now, I'm only interested in one player."

"Who?" Julie asked, finally catching her breath. Boy, was it ever snowing, and the winds were really kicking up.

"The wife of Davy's brother. Come on."

Bethany gazed at the lazy river and stopped. Pine Lakes

was a family community. Beautiful. Cozy. Quaint. How had such a beautiful work of art become such a dark nightmare?

"When I was a little girl, my daddy used to bring us to the diner standing behind us. We would order a cheeseburger and a milkshake. After we ate, Daddy would walk me down to this river. We would sit right over there." Bethany raised a gloved hand and pointed to a fallen log. "Daddy and I would sit on that log for hours and talk. I can't remember everything we talked about, but it was so special. Sometimes I forget about the times Daddy and I spent together. One of the most special times I spent with Daddy was in Snow Falls. That's why I moved to Snow Falls."

Julie stepped up to Bethany. "Love, are you alright?"

"Oh, suddenly I'm wondering when the dark clouds are going to fade away. But right now," Bethany drew in a deep breath of cold air, "we need to go find a missing wife."

"Maybe we better contact Sheriff Murphy?" Julie suggested. "Love, this scene is getting far too dangerous. A man has been kidnapped—"

"Julie, if I don't play along, my mother will die," Bethany informed Julie in a tone that caused her friend to nearly lose all hope. "I don't have a choice...and I'm thinking that Ralph Polonzio is hoping that I'm smarter than he realizes. The snake gave me a bunch of tattered information, but I sensed that he's got a weight on his own shoulders that's connected to more than just money."

Julie felt a million question marks pop into her confused mind. Whatever Bethany was talking about was obviously important.

"Okay, love, it's time for me to play catch-up. What do we do in the meantime?"

"Go find a missing wife."

Bethany grabbed Julie's arm and hurried away from the river. As she did, a middle-aged woman stepped out of the diner, looked around, and spotted Bethany and Julie hurrying away into the snow. She pulled a cellphone out of a gray coat pocket and made a call.

"Yes, I need to speak to Sheriff Murphy. The call is very urgent!"

Sheriff Murphy answered the call and was quickly pulled into a dark web of danger and murder.

chapter thirteen

Justine Gray heard the front doorbell to her house chime through her home. She slowly lowered a cup of coffee and looked through a comfortably sized kitchen filled with fancy appliances.

Her right hand released the coffee cup she was holding and slid over to a sleeping Glock 17 sitting mere inches away. A security monitor was resting on a back counter. Justine eyed the kitchen and then quickly grabbed her gun, backed away from a glossy wooden table, and made her way across a gray marble floor. The security monitor showed two snow-soaked women standing on a frozen front porch.

"Bethany Lights...Julie Walsh...what are they doing here?"

Panic gripped Justine's mind. Deep down in her heart, Justine knew she had dived into a deep end of a deadly pool that was preparing a vicious grave for her. What had begun as a simple plan to get revenge on Tracy Bates and Richard Gray had turned into a nightmare. Tracy Bates had proven to be a tough woman to control and destroy. If Justine had known that her opponent had been involved with so many dangerous people, she would have backed down and simply divorced her unfaithful husband.

Justine lowered her eyes and fixed them on the gun she was holding. Could she kill Bethany and Julie? Only time would tell.

"Alright." Justine quickly made sure her short black hair was standing still in its updo and brushed at the fancy gray suit she was wearing. "Alright."

"Maybe she's not home?" Julie suggested to Bethany.

Bethany glanced toward a two-car garage attached to a lovely two-story home. The garage door was pulled open. A blue BMW sat in the garage all alone. A spot reserved for a second vehicle was empty.

"The license plate on that car has the word 'Educator' on it. I think Justine Gray is home."

Julie looked around. A snow-covered middle-class neighborhood stood all around her. "Maybe we should start a taxi business?" she suggested, speaking through a hard falling snow. "I never realized the taxi business paid off so well."

"It doesn't." Bethany bit down on her lower lip and rang the glowing front doorbell button again.

"I'm coming...hold on..." Justine rushed through a large living room filled with luxurious furnishings that complemented soft cranberry-colored walls. "Hold on."

Bethany made sure her daddy's old gun was secured in the right pocket of her coat while Julie stepped close.

"Follow my lead, honey," she whispered.

"I will." Julie stiffened some. She wasn't sure what to expect. Maybe a nightmare...or maybe a simple cup of hot coffee?

Justine stopped at a hardwood front door with two rectangular stained-glass windows perched on both sides of its arms. Bracing herself for the unknown, she quickly forced her heart to slow down and her mind to take firm control over every action that needed to be fulfilled.

"Do what needs to be done." Justine reached out her right hand, disengaged a glowing alarm system pad, crippled a heavy deadbolt lock, and eased open the front door. Two snow-covered women appeared behind a glass storm door.

"Yes? Can I help you?" she asked, pretending not to know who Bethany or Julie was.

"Mrs. Gray?" Bethany called through the door.

Justine pitched an eye behind Bethany. She spotted a heavy snow falling onto a silent, sleepy neighborhood.

"Yes?"

"My name is Bethany Lights. This is my friend Julie Walsh. Perhaps you know who we are? If you do, perhaps we can help each other?" Bethany asked carefully.

"I don't know who you are."

"Mrs. Gray, do the names Tracy Bates, Ralph Polonzio, Tony Polonzio, Mr. Marizzo, or Walley Griffin ring a bell? Do the names Patrick Brakemyer and Brad Griffin ring a bell? Those two men are dead." Bethany stared through the frosted glass door, struggling to see Justine. "Mrs. Gray, I have a bad feeling you're in trouble. Please, perhaps we can help each other? I know my friend and I are supposed to be dead, but maybe if we help each other, we might all live."

Justine felt her heart hit a cold marble floor. Her hands shook and desperate tears flooded from her eyes, scarring the mascara she was wearing. Without understanding why, she unlocked the storm door and threw it open.

"Inside, hurry," she begged.

Bethany grabbed Julie's hand and hurried into a brightly lit foyer. Justine slammed the storm door and closed the front door without wasting a second. Bethany and Julie stepped back and watched the woman reactivate an alarm system with trembling hands.

"Mrs. Gray—"

"The kitchen please."

Justine took off toward the kitchen like a scalded cat. Bethany and Julie exchanged uneasy glances, but cautiously followed.

"It's not what you think," Justine spoke in a tearful voice when Bethany and Julie appeared in the kitchen. "I didn't want matters to turn out like this. Everything got out of control." She lifted the back of a gray long-sleeve blouse, pulled out a deadly gun, and continued. "I lost control," she told Bethany and Julie as she placed the gun she was holding down next to a silver toaster oven resting on a gray granite countertop. She stared at the gun through scared tears and turned to face the two women standing in her kitchen. "I'm not a killer. I admit I told myself a million times I'll kill anyone who threatens me. But I...I can't..."

Bethany reached into her right coat pocket and retrieved her daddy's old gun. She walked over to a lovely kitchen table and set the gun down.

"Mrs. Gray, we're not here to harm you or anyone else. I promise. This is the only gun my friend and I have." Bethany pushed the gun across the kitchen table, out of reach. "Ralph Polonzio approached me while I was standing outside the Pine Lakes Diner. I don't think I've ever had the displeasure of meeting a more disgusting human being in my life. That awful man told me quite a lot, but I could sense that he was twisting many truths to fit his own agenda."

"Ralph Polonzio is a liar!" Justine exclaimed. "Don't believe a word that filthy piece of fish bait tells you!"

Bethany detected a thick New York accent hiding under Justine's voice. *Davy never told me where the rehab center his brother attended is located. Where did Richard Gray meet his wife? I detect a New York accent. Hmmm…*

Bethany pushed every distracting thought out of her mind and focused directly on Justine.

"Mrs. Gray, may I ask you where you are from? I detect a New York accent."

"I'm from Brooklyn," Justine cut Bethany off. "And yes, before you ask, Ralph Polonzio is my cousin, and so is Tony Polonzio. Happy?"

"No," Bethany said honestly. "I want to know what's truly going on, Mrs. Gray. I want the truth. Please. Our lives are at stake."

"Please," Julie spoke up in a soft, pleading voice. "Mrs. Gray, we can help each other."

"Can we?" Justine asked through her tears. She looked down at the gun lying next to a sleepy toaster oven. "Maybe I should just kill myself and end this misery, huh?"

"Suicide isn't the answer, Mrs. Gray." Bethany pulled out an expensive kitchen chair and sat down. "Talk to me. Please."

"What's to talk about? My husband was being unfaithful with Tracy Bates. I found out the truth, and I was determined to destroy Tracy Bates. I was determined to make the woman suffer." Justine wiped her tears. "Instead of attacking Tracy, I forced myself to become her closest and dearest friend. I earned her trust. I found out her secrets...well, most of them. In time, I took Tracy to New York. My intention was to hire Ralph to...kill her. Only Ralph ruined everything!" Justine hollered. "That awful snake let his eyes fall for Tracy's evil beauty. Tracy began taking regular trips to New York, and Ralph betrayed me. The only good part of all this is that Tracy got herself in trouble with a bookie who doesn't like to be cheated, and then rubbed a deadly man the wrong way."

"Mr. Marizzo?" Bethany asked.

Justine nodded. "That's the man. Mr. Marizzo is a man that even the FBI backs away from, if you catch my drift. He's not associated with the mafia, but he grew up killing for the mafia in real bad ways." Justine crossed her arms. "Tracy, Ralph, Tony...everybody started stabbing each other in the back. I had to play along because Richard—that's my no-good husband—he's a heavy drug dealer. I always look the other way. And why not? Look at my home. I drive a BMW, and Richard paid my way through college."

"Mrs. Gray, we're not here to judge you," Bethany promised.

"It seems like you're doing a good job of that already," Julie pointed out.

Justine snapped her eyes at Julie. "And why shouldn't I? I know Patrick Brakemyer is dead. That poor guy...he was playing Ralph, but he was giving me information almost every week. He's the reason I could keep up with all the twists and turns. Patrick married my cousin. He was such a sweet guy, so smart. But he always had something to prove. That's the way of it when you live in Brooklyn." Justine wiped her tears. "I was the one who asked Patrick to come to Pine Lakes. He's dead because of me."

Bethany settled back in her chair. Instead of allowing confusion to dictate her thinking, she kept her mind focused entirely on Justine. *Okay, this woman's story relates to the story Ralph Polonzio told me, maybe verse per verse. But there is a connection. So now what?*

"Mrs. Gray, Ralph Polonzio told me that my mother is hiding millions in cash at the lake house up on Old Wolf Mountain."

"Oh, if only your mother hadn't left her pocketbook behind!" Justine could have clawed the air in half with her fingernails. "I like your mother, Ms. Lights. She's a decent-hearted woman. When I saw she had left her pocketbook behind after a meeting, I picked it up, but the strap broke. All the contents went spilling out onto the floor."

"That's when you spotted my mother's financial ledger?" Bethany asked.

"Yes," Justine nodded. "I'm the one who helped get Tracy Bates hired on as principal at Pine Lakes Elementary, and then I set her up for a hard fall. I hoped to destroy her reputation and force her to leave Pine Lakes. Ralph, Tony, my husband...everyone was running around in this confusing maze. I thought if I could just force Tracy Bates to leave Pine Lakes, I could get a grip on matters. But as I was picking up your mother's belongings, Tracy appeared behind me. She spotted your mother's financial ledger before I could place it back into your mother's pocketbook. Tracy snatched the ledger from my hands before I could stop her."

"What happened?" Bethany asked.

Justine struggled to calm down. "The meeting in question was one of many that was to determine if Tracy was going to get fired or not. Tracy wasn't aware that I was the person who had leaked damaging information to your mother and to other members of the board members. She was furious. When she began going through your mother's ledger..." Justine shook her head. "Ms. Lights, the ledger in question had evidence that your mother had been withdrawing sizeable sums of money over a period of many years and hiding the money at the lake house. Beside each financial entry, she wrote the words 'Money at Lake House.' And because your mother was the one who demanded Tracy's resignation, and because by then Tracy was in very serious financial trouble...you do the math."

"I will, eventually. But may I ask, did you tell Patrick Brakemyer about the money?" Bethany asked.

"Of course I did. Patrick was risking his life to help me. I wouldn't dare keep anything from him. My cousin married last month. I think he rushed into the marriage because he was afraid he might end up dead and never have a wife. The situation turned intense after Tracy discovered your mother's secret."

I still can't believe Mother would hide millions in cold cash at the lake house. Mother doesn't even have millions to hide away. Yes, I come from a wealthy family, but not that wealthy. Why in the world would mother keep such a strange financial ledger? I'll have to find out later.

"Justine, what does Ralph Polonzio really want? Why do you think he approached me and demanded I help him find the money, then threatened to kill my mother if I refused?"

"Because he's desperate," Justine declared. "Ralph is a vicious cocaine user. He's also a vicious drinker. During his sober periods, he's able to think and wise up some. Right now, he knows Tracy and Tony want him dead, and he knows Richard has left the scene, leaving him high and dry. He knows Mr. Marizzo wants to make him eat a bullet. Ralph is desperate."

"Where is your husband?" Bethany asked.

A disgusted scowl formed on Justine's beautiful face. "My husband ran off like the coward he is. He took our money and vanished. I'm guessing he's driving toward California as we speak. Poor Davy...he's the only decent person in this scenario. Tracy only married him because she was always attracted to Richard. Oh, it's a long, ugly story."

"Ralph told me about a plan to kill Davy and plant the murder on your husband." Bethany continued to question Justine, avoiding stepping off onto a side trail.

"Tracy's idea. I had to play along. Tracy still thinks I'm on her side...at least, I believe she does." Justine hurried over to the kitchen table and sat down across from Bethany. "Ralph called me earlier. He told me to stay here at the house and threatened to kill me if I tried to leave—he meant his words. I was so stupid to take Tracy to New York. I was blinded by absolute rage. Believe it or not, I loved my husband...until I discovered the truth." Justine wiped at another set of stinging tears. "I don't know what's going on. I don't know where Tracy is. All I know is that Richard left late last night. He cleared out the bank accounts and left, then Ralph called me. That's the truth."

Bethany stared into a pair of terrified, panicked eyes that

needed a friend, and not an enemy. "Mrs. Gray, I think everyone in question just might be up at the lake house on Old Wolf Mountain...and I fear that all the players are still determined to catch the king." She rubbed her eyes with a tired hand. "Mrs. Gray, please make a pot of coffee because we have a lot of thinking to do."

chapter fourteen

"**P**erfect!" Tracy Bates widened her soulless eyes. "They're in the house, Richard."

Richard Gray nodded. "They'll join him," he promised Tracy, tossing a thumb over his shoulder. A dead body was lying in the back of a white work van that had the words "Gray Electrical" written on the side of it in bright green letters. A little cartoon man holding two electrical wires stood smiling under the words. "Tony Polonzio is dead. I wish the killing would stop."

Tracy turned and looked at the man who held the rough image of an ex-Green Beret. Richard Gray was handsome, rugged, and rougher than a wild grizzly—at least, in certain aspects. Deep down, the man feared Mr. Marizzo...and so did Tracy.

Richard wasn't stupid. He knew that Mr. Marizzo carried an insane, bloody mind inside his head. The man would dedicate himself to tracking down Richard no matter how long it took—and no matter the cost. The only chance Richard had to stay alive was to kill off his enemies.

Tracy knew how the playing field was set up. She was fully aware that Richard was now in attack mode—survival mode, really—and she was fully on board.

"Keep Bethany Lights alive. We need her."

"I don't see why we're wasting our time with her. Why don't we grab Rachel Lights and make her talk?" Richard grumbled. His body was hungering for a line of white powder. He turned his head and looked at a black widow spider who appeared as a very attractive blond-haired woman. She was wearing a bright pink snow suit, pink lip stick, and pink nail polish. Richard didn't mind all the pink. He thought the pink flattered Tracy's features. Davy, his rotten brother, hated the pink. But what did Davy know?

"How are you doing back there, Davy, huh?"

Davy couldn't answer. A mountain of gray duct tape was wrapped around his mouth. His arms and legs were also duct-taped to a flimsy wooden chair sitting beside a dead body.

"Richard, I know Mrs. Lights. The old woman is very stubborn. I don't believe she would talk. You should have seen the way she decimated my character at the school board meeting. No, it would be smarter to go for the daughter. Bethany Lights is weak."

"Bethany Lights is a smart dame," Ralph called out from the back of the van.

Davy moved his eyes and saw Ralph sitting on a box filled with old wires. Ralph had his right hand wrapped around a sour liquor bottle. "Maybe she fell for my act, and maybe she didn't?" he said to Richard and Tracy, and then took a deep swig of whiskey.

"I don't see why you even talked to her." Richard folded a pair of large arms over a black coat. "I would have killed her and went for the old lady."

"Well, you're not us, are you, smart-mouth?" Ralph snapped at Richard. "Tracy and me put a plan together. We wanted the dame to chase her tail some and follow her. She might know more than we think she knows. And lo and behold, stupid, the dame ran right to your wife. Now we'll see where they go. To the cops? Maybe, maybe not. All we know is that Mr. Marizzo is out to kill us all, and that's not going to happen. Mr. Marizzo has gone invisible, and that's not good."

"I still don't understand why you just didn't kill Bethany Lights and her friend. I could have killed Julie—"

"Honey." Tracy reached over an icy hand and touched Richard's shoulder. "Walley Griffin is still alive. Mr. Marizzo is missing...well, he's not letting himself be seen. Your wife is a liability—that awful traitor. I assumed she was my friend."

"Hey, no one is your friend, Tracy. How many times do I have to tell you that? If it wasn't for me, Justine Gray would have swallowed you whole," Ralph spat at Tracy. "Now listen, the both of you, we don't need a bunch of dead bodies in this town! You hear me! I plugged Tony, but that was personal because no one stabs Ralph Polonzio in the back and gets away with it. But Tony is the only one that dies today. As for you"—Ralph raised a hard foot and kicked Davy— "you'll be taken care of later...out of town. Right now, we need to see what everyone knows. I done told you that Bethany Lights is a smart dame. I found the book she wrote, and way up there in the frozen land, she's done been involved with some serious murders. There's no telling what she knows or don't know, or who she might have talked to. We need to be smart and watch! You hear me?"

"Ralph is right," Tracy spoke to Richard in a sleazy voice that was supposed to sound supportive and caring. "This situation has spiraled out of control, Richard, but we still have a chance to make it."

Richard shook his head. "Tracy, you must be insane to think we can win this fight. We need to make a run for it. There's too many loose ends, I'm telling you." He unfolded his arms and ran an angry hand through a head of graying black hair. "Walley Griffin messed everything up. I told you not to trust that guy. If he and his brother would have done what they were told—"

"Hey, stop barking your mouth and shut up!" Ralph roared. "What's done is done. Tracy hired two clowns by mistake. It happens."

"Richard, my plan was perfect," Tracy insisted. "Davy's death was going to be blamed on Justine. Julie Walsh was going to be the tool that cracked Bethany Lights's mouth open for us. I'm sorry Walley betrayed us. I honestly thought I had him under my control. I was only trying to keep the scene private. That's why I wanted everything to take place up on the mountain. We were going to ditch the bodies in the lake after everything was said and done."

"If I had been there—"

"Well, you weren't there were you, smart-mouth?" Ralph asked. "Tracy made everyone think she was in Raleigh, but she was in New York with you and me because we had a meeting with Mr. Marizzo. We got delayed and missed our flight back down here to the woods...it happens. What can you do? We got to the scene later than we wanted to. Now we have to deal with a jar of spilled pennies."

"Mr. Marizzo..." Richard shook his head. "Tracy, that man intends to kill us all. You heard what he said to us at the meeting. You saw the way he was looking at us...with those snake eyes."

Tracy Bates wanted to object, but she couldn't. She felt nearly paralyzed with fear. What had begun as a simple plan had backfired and somehow twisted into a series of complicated mazes that her desperate mind couldn't navigate.

"We need the money, Richard," she finally snapped, losing her patience with the man she supposedly loved. Did Tracy Bates love Richard? Of course not, the woman couldn't love anyone other than herself. Richard ran drugs for Mr. Marizzo, a man Ralph had introduced him to. For many years, the drug operation had run so smoothly that Tracy became overly confident that no one could stand in her way. After moving to Pine Lakes with Davy—against her will—it wasn't long before Tracy learned that Richard and his darling wife had both worked their way through a drug rehab center. Tracy, who was young and daring—and addicted to cocaine— approached Richard alone one day and began a little...flirting...and then offered the man some white powder. Why? Tracy could tell Richard was struggling to remain sober, struggling to work for his loser brother as an electrician's helper. Tracy quickly broke Richard with her looks and desire to control him. Shortly after that, she talked Richard into starting a lousy cab business, and from there, the drugs rolled in.

For many years, life had been good...great. But somehow, Justine had discovered the truth—or maybe the woman had always known the truth and looked the other way? Maybe the idea of drugs didn't bother her? But maybe the idea that her husband was being unfaithful did. Tracy wasn't certain. All Tracy knew was that even though life had been good in Pine Lakes, in New York, she had created a mess for herself. High gambling debts had piled up...dangerously high gambling debts. On top of that concern, Mr. Marizzo was growing impatient running drugs through Pine Lakes and was preparing to move on, which meant the people involved with the drugs being run through Pine Lakes had to eat a bullet.

When Ralph had informed Tracy that her dearest friend was preparing to betray her, that was the straw that broke the camel's back. Tracy went into attack mode. Only, her carefully created plan had backfired right in her face. Justice was beautiful.

"I know Mr. Marizzo is planning to kill us, Richard. I'm not blind!" Tracy snapped again, allowing her hard, evil heart to peek through her eyes. "We should have killed Justine."

"No," Richard objected. "Tracy, I made my point clear on

that. Justine is innocent in all this. I feel bad for betraying her trust."

Deep down, Richard wished Tracy Bates had never been born. But like the drugs he was now enslaved to, Richard was now also enslaved to Tracy. He couldn't break free from the woman. He was addicted.

"Davy, I'm sorry about this. But you put your nose in where it didn't belong. If only you would have looked the other way."

Davy narrowed a pair of angry eyes. Sure, he had lied to Bethany and Julie. Davy knew everything that was taking place behind the scenes. He had approached Bethany's mother after picking the woman up from the airport and worked for her. Why not? Davy had an excellent reputation in town, and everyone Rachel Lights spoke to give Davy an outstanding reference. Once Davy got on her good side, he went to work to save his life and take out everyone who wanted him dead.

The one bullet that took Davy down was that he had not been aware that his deadly ex-wife had hired Walley and Brad Griffin. When Brad Griffin had attacked his cab and allowed Davy to leave...well, Davy assumed he had been shot at and chased back to the house by either Tracy and his brother, or maybe Ralph or even Tony? Tracy was playing Tony Polonzio like a broken fiddle—the slug didn't stand a chance with Tracy. When Walley Griffin appeared on the scene, Davy had been tossed into a pit of confusion. New players were on the scene. How? Who were they? What did it all mean? When Davy had spotted Tracy's nail polish on an old doorknob, he knew.

"Look." Tracy pointed down a snowy street. "Here they come!"

Richard glanced at the snowy road. He spotted Bethany, Julie, and Justine coming out of the front door of his house. He quickly ducked down. Tracy followed.

"Davy lives right across the street," Justine spoke quickly. "There's one of his work vans."

Bethany looked across the street and spotted another snow-covered two-story home. A white work van was sitting in a frozen driveway covered with deep snow. For all intents and purposes, the work van appeared as if it had been sitting out in the elements untouched for weeks. But something about the van caught Bethany's eye. *The snow...there's no snow on the front windshield.*

"I don't see anyone out here, Justine. I think we're okay for now. Let's get back inside. We're not safe in the open like this."

The tone of Bethany's voice threw Julie into action. She reached out and grabbed Justine's hand.

"Come on, love, we're not safe out here. No one may be peeking at us right now, but who knows?" Julie gave Justine an urgent glance.

"What? Oh, well..."

Bethany motioned around with her left hand. "Justine, there's no one out here. I don't know what you heard. It was probably the wind. Now let's get back inside." She grabbed Justine's other hand and hurriedly walked the woman back into her home. Once inside, she closed the front door.

"Someone is sitting in the work van across the street," she told Justine and ran into a fancy living room.

"The work van? Impossible. I've been home all morning. I would have seen—"

"The work van is backed up to the garage door. Anyone could have crawled into the back door of the van without being seen." Bethany rushed over to a front window covered by a light blue drape. Behind the drape, expensive wooden blinds lay closed. Bethany peeled back the edge of the drape and then, as if she were handling a live bomb, eased down part of a wooden blind just enough to see outside. The front window was iced over, but Bethany could just make out the work van sitting across the street. *I'm not dealing with a group of Einsteins, that's for sure.*

"What do you see, love?" Julie asked, stepping close to Bethany.

"It's hard to see. The window is iced over, but I can see the work van." Bethany let go of the blind. "The van is a blur. I need a better view." She looked around. "I'll be right back. Stay here," she told everyone, and then burst out of the living room and made her way to the kitchen. Without skipping a beat, she snatched up her daddy's old gun, as well as Justine's gun, and slipped out of the back door. She fought her way to the corner of the house just in time to see two heads appear in the front of the work van.

"If the windshield of that van had been covered with snow, I would not even have looked twice. Right now, Julie and I would be walking Justine to the sheriff's office. Who knows what would have happened?" *The only question is, what do I do now? Do I call Sheriff Murphy?*

Before Bethany could finish her thoughts, a cold, hard hand grabbed her shoulder. Bethany was spun around in her tracks and forced to look into the face of two deadly thugs standing in front of a seventy-year-old man wearing a deep, vicious frown.

"We need to talk," Mr. Marizzo spoke to Bethany in a tone that clearly informed the poor woman that she was dead meat.

chapter fifteen

A rough hand that belonged to a tall, ugly, pizza-faced thug shoved Bethany back into Justine's kitchen. Julie and Justine were both standing in the kitchen when Bethany appeared.

"Bethany—"

"Everyone sit down," Mr. Marizzo ordered, stepping into the kitchen behind his thug. He brushed snow off his expensive gray overcoat and removed an old fedora hat.

"Do what he says," Bethany said calmly.

"I ain't here to kill you," Mr. Marizzo informed everyone, waiting as his hosts all took a seat. "It's like this: I know my rats are across the street. I got my guys everywhere. What I don't need is interference. So it's like this: I'll take care of the rats if you back off. If you don't...maybe I'll put your head in a vice?" Mr. Marizzo spoke with a deep Italian-Brooklyn accent that was difficult to understand. "Besides, there's one more rat up at your house," he told Bethany. "They all thought I was stupid or something. I've been handling the rats ever since they took my cheese. Tracy Bates ain't nothing, and neither is your husband. Ralph and Tony? Forget about them —small-time change. I let them run my drugs because I have a friend who lives down here in the woods. We go way back, and he has an operation. Pine Lakes was useful." He scanned the kitchen. "It's like this, you understand: friend or no friend, when a rat becomes a threat, you kill it. Capeesh?"

"Mr. Marizzo—" Justine pleaded.

"Shut your mouth when I'm speaking," Mr. Marizzo warned Justine, who winced and hushed. "I ain't here to kill you. I don't care about your mother's money, either. I got all the money I need. I was giving all my rats time to sweat it out while getting caught in their own traps. You heard me." Mr. Marizzo pulled a half-smoked cigar from his coat pocket. "Patrick Brakemyer was working for me. I told him who to talk to and who not to talk to. That's why I let him talk to you," he nodded at Justine. "That's why I let him play Ralph for me. I wanted everyone to fall into their own traps and start sweating. Why? Sometimes you got to let the rats sweat some to see the real poison inside of them."

Bethany slowly placed her hands together. She still had two guns in her pocket. Did Mr. Marizzo know about the guns? She didn't want to ask. The thug standing next to the old man resembled a soulless killer who had sent many men to their graves.

"Mr. Marizzo, what do you want us to do?"

"I want you to forget about everything," Mr. Marizzo told Bethany, speaking in a clear and direct tone. "You go handle Walley Griffin. He's up at your house, thinking he's some kind of wise guy. I had my daughter call the local sheriff and lead him off on a wild goose chase."

"Why?" Bethany asked.

"Because I don't like the law!" Mr. Marizzo nearly spat out his cigar. "Now listen to me—Walley Griffin is your chore. I'll handle my own rats. You understand me? What happens between you and Walley Griffin is your business. Walley Griffin don't know nothing about me. If you don't take care of him, he'll go after your mother. Family business is family business, understand? Walley Griffin made it personal. When it's personal, you handle matters yourself. Why do you think I'm here?"

"Alright, Mr. Marizzo, I'll handle Walley Griffin," Bethany nodded. "But please, if you find Davy Gray, don't—"

"Davy Gray is in the back of that van parked across the street. I'll be sending him your way. What? Do you think I was going to send you back up the mountain alone?" Mr. Marizzo shook his head. "You think I'm stupid? You think that pitiful six shooter and pop gun in your coat pockets can save you? Let me tell you something—Walley Griffin ain't stupid. He's smarter than the rats I'm gonna kill today. You gonna need Davy Gray. Davy Gray, he ain't such a bad guy...just got caught up in the wrong winds is all. I ain't hard on people who get trapped against by mistake. What, do you think I'm heartless?"

"As a matter of fact, I do," Bethany offered an honest answer. Julie and Justine both tensed up and prepared to be shot dead on the spot.

Mr. Marizzo shrugged his shoulders. "Maybe you're right," he told Bethany. "But I'm also a man who doesn't like to kill innocent people. Understand me?" He narrowed a pair of deadly eyes. "Go handle Walley Griffin. End this for yourself, and then walk away. Far away."

"Is that what you really want, Mr. Marizzo?" Bethany asked. "Are you really going to let us live?"

Mr. Marizzo lifted a rough hand and removed the cigar from his mouth. "If you want to live, do as I say," he warned Bethany. "May the best man win, cuz Walley Griffin ain't gonna be easy to kill. Maybe he'll take you out for me? Maybe that's what I want, huh? Or maybe I want you to kill him? If you kill Walley Griffin, remember to keep your stupid mouth shut because I know where you live in Snow Falls." He stepped close to the kitchen table. "Conrad Spencer was a detective in New York years back. He saved my life once. I owe him. I called him and told him about you.

We had a little talk. He cashed in on the only favor I'm ever gonna give him. Count your blessings and be happy I'm letting you live and have a go at Walley Griffin. Understand?"

Bethany nodded. "I understand, Mr. Marizzo. When you leave this kitchen, your name will never leave my lips ever again. I'll scourge your image out of my mind with bleach."

"You do that." Mr. Marizzo nodded at his hired thug. "Let's go."

Bethany sat still and watched Mr. Marizzo leave the kitchen. As soon as the kitchen door closed, shooting erupted from across the street. Justine tried to stand up, but Bethany told her to remain still. Julie closed her eyes as if she were preparing to go down a steep hill on a rollercoaster.

Outside in the snow, four armed men filled the front of the van full of bullets. Tracy Bates and Richard Gray were shot dead before they could move. Ralph attempted to flee out the back door of the van but was met by a hurricane of sizzling bullets that ended his miserable life. Seconds later, a man wearing a black ski suit and a black ski mask appeared in the back of the van and cut Davy loose.

"You saw nothing. Now get across the street. Your friends are waiting for you. Use the back door, wise guy," the man ordered Davy in a thick Brooklyn accent before he vanished back into the snow.

Davy looked toward the front of the van. He saw a pair of limp arms dangling from two dead bodies.

"Richard...why?" he moaned, and then scrambled out into the snow. Ralph was lying dead on the ground a few feet from the back of the van. Davy scanned the snow but didn't see anyone, and then he ran across the street and made his way to the back door of his brother's house. He threw the kitchen door open and saw Bethany, Julie, and Justine sitting at a miserable kitchen table that no longer appeared cozy or welcoming.

"Richard's dead, isn't he?" Justine asked through a flood of tears.

Davy closed the back door with a shaky hand. "Yeah. he's dead. So are Tracy Bates and Ralph Polonzio." Davy walked over to the kitchen table and put a sad hand on Justine's shoulder. "I'm sorry, Justine. I was trying to handle all this." Davy glanced at Bethany and Julie. "I'm sorry I lied. But the truth is, I really didn't know what was happening up at the lake house."

Bethany didn't become upset with Davy. "Mr. Marizzo told us that Walley Griffin is waiting for us at the lake house. We were ordered to handle him." She slowly stood up, reached into the right pocket of her coat, and pulled out Justine's gun. "Here, Davy."

Davy accepted the gun with a deflated hand. "I'll call Sheriff Murphy."

"No need," said another voice.

Bethany spun around. Riley was standing in the doorway to the kitchen wearing a hard face.

"Sheriff Murphy—"

"Before you ask what I'm doing here, let me just say that after I found out Paulie Marizzo was involved in this mess, I backed down and let the man handle his own," he said. "You don't rub a man like Paulie Marizzo the wrong way." He removed a snow-covered sheriff's hat. "I thought I was a decent cop, but all this time, drugs have been running through this town." Riley looked down at the sheriff's badge attached to the outside of his brown coat. He shook his head, and with a tired hand, removed the badge. "Years back, I was flying a transport plane. I was in the navy then. The plane took on a serious engine problem. I couldn't handle the plane. My co-pilot and I tried to land the plane in a field...we hit hard. My co-pilot was killed on contact and three other people died...good men with families. I've never forgiven myself for the crash, and now look: I let drugs be run through my town. How many people have I harmed because I didn't do my job?"

"Sheriff." Bethany stood up and walked over to Riley. *So he is human after all. Good.* "You're only one man. Now put back on your badge. We have to go trap Walley Griffin." Before Riley could say a word, Bethany pressed his badge back against his coat. "Put your badge back on and do your job," she spoke in a stern but caring tone. "We're only human, and we're far from perfect."

"Bethany is right, Riley. I had a notion about Richard, but I turned a blind eye. I didn't want to accept the truth until it was too late." Davy shook his head. "Richard was my brother."

Riley looked into Bethany's eyes and then over at Davy. "Maybe I wanted to accept the fact that I was running a quiet little town. Maybe I didn't want to kick over a few rocks myself. Maybe I wanted to sit around and feel sorry for myself." He looked down at his badge. "Alright, Ms. Lights." He nodded and returned the badge to his coat. "I have a job to do."

Bethany watched Riley walk over to a kitchen phone and make a call. "Donald, we had a shooting. Get all our guys over to Baker's Street. Have Fred use the plow to lead the way. Hurry." He ended the call with a hard hand. "Davy, my job is here. I saw a snowmobile in the garage."

"I'll be up on the mountain before it gets dark," Davy promised. He turned to Bethany and nodded toward the kitchen door. "There's another snowmobile parked in my garage across the street. Well, it *was* my garage."

"Julie and I will be right behind you," Bethany promised. "Justine, you're going to stay here with Sheriff Murphy."

Riley agreed. "And don't worry, I know who all the dirty players are, Mrs. Gray. I spoke to Wanda Brakemyer. Mrs. Brakemyer turned over a great deal of information to me that her husband had collected before his death. You're going to be alright." He focused on Bethany. "I'm supposed to be on a wild goose chase right now. Maybe in the end, I'll have a little talk with Mr. Marizzo and show him the evidence I have. Maybe Mr. Marizzo and I can come to some kind of agreement that will keep him out of Pine Lakes for good."

"How awful is all of this!" Julie finally spoke in a voice that flashed with anger. "My goodness, this is the worst!" She stood up suddenly. "Love," she told Bethany, "the next time someone calls and threatens me...well, I'll just let that person come to Snow Falls and fight it out there. It's not safe anywhere else."

Before anyone could say anything, a secured cell phone Riley was carrying came to life. He checked and answered the call.

"Yeah, right here." He held out the cell phone to Bethany. "It's Sarah Spencer."

Bethany winced and braced herself for a scolding.

"Hello, Sarah," she breathed.

"The man who called Julie Walsh was a friend of her ex-husband's," Sarah spoke in a professional tone. "I got all of Julie's cell phone records and tracked the call. The London police now have the man who threatened Julie in custody and her ex-husband isn't any better off."

"Oh...well, Sarah, that's wonderful news. I—"

"Mr. Marizzo is a dangerous man, Bethany. He called Conrad's phone and let Conrad hear a good amount of shooting. What happened?" Sarah demanded.

Bethany closed her eyes. "Mr. Marizzo killed off his enemies and left me to go find one last rat."

"Walley Griffin."

"Yes, how did you know? Well, maybe I shouldn't ask. Sarah, I'm sorry. I should have told you that someone threatened Julie. I didn't want to...well, that's not important now. I'm sorry." Bethany felt awful. Sarah was cleaning up her mess.

"For what?" Sarah asked, keeping her voice in detective mode. "Listen to me, Bethany. I have little on Walley Griffin. He's been arrested four times in the last two years for assault. He was released from the navy for hitting an officer and nearly went to prison for murder soon after his release, but the prosecution botched up the evidence. Walley Griffin is a hostile target. Be careful."

"Sarah...you mean..."

"Bethany, Mr. Marizzo told Conrad that he's sending you at Walley Griffin. Do you know what that means?" Sarah's voice grew stern. "It means for a man like Mr. Marizzo that you either kill our target or you're going to be killed. I don't know what Mr. Marizzo told you, Bethany, but unless Walley Griffin goes down, you're a dead woman. It's as simple as that. He'll be watching."

"I don't understand," Bethany confessed. *I can barely understand any of this.*

"It's the way of the mafia, Bethany. Don't believe for one second that Mr. Marizzo is a stupid man," Sarah continued. "Take Walley Griffin down regardless of what Mr. Marizzo told you. People like that can manipulate clear intention with deceitful whispers."

"Alright, Sarah. The ball is in my court."

"Yes, honey, the ball is in your court. And Bethany? I have confidence in your ability."

With those affirming words, Sarah ended the call.

chapter sixteen

Cold, blistering snow stung Bethany's face. She feared her face might turn into a solid block of ice by the time she reached the lake house.

Julie wasn't any better off; both women were frozen through and through. To make matters worse, night had fallen, dragging down a black marble darkness from a storm-sick sky that showed no signs of abating.

"We're...here..." Bethany whispered through chattering teeth as she peeled her body off an expensive blue and silver snowmobile.

"Are...we even alive...love?" Julie asked, struggling to feel her legs.

Davy parked his snowmobile, jumped off, and hurried over to his friends.

"Okay, we're about a mile south from the house. We'll follow the river north and get close. You ladies did good getting up here. I'm impressed at how you handled the snowmobile, Bethany."

"Don't be." Bethany touched her face with two gloved hands. A heavy green ski mask covered her face. Well, the ski mask had once been green, but now it was white from the snow. "Remind me to move to the moon after this."

"Me too," Julie whimpered. The green ski mask she was wearing was also white from the snow. "I love the cold and snow, but there comes a time when a gal needs a hot tea and a crumpet."

"I guess so." Davy felt sorry for Bethany and Julie. Both women were being so brave. "Maybe you should stay here. I can go after Walley Griffin." He dismounted a powerful hunting rifle from his shoulder.

"No. We're a team." Bethany worked her fingers back and forth for a minute, hoping to bring life back into them, and scanned a dark river. "Alright, Davy, lead the way. Julie and I will follow."

"Stay close," Davy ordered, and then turned away and started walking north. Bethany and Julie both followed on uncertain legs.

Davy braced himself against the storm and forced his way through knee-deep snow, one painful step at a time. Every so often, he glanced back to make sure Bethany and Julie were still behind him, expecting the women to have fallen back. Each time, he spotted two daring women struggling through the snow mere inches from his heels.

He kept walking north until the river began hugging the edge of the mountain road. The river, he knew, hugged the side of the mountain road about a quarter mile from the house and dived back into the woods.

"Almost to the house," he announced.

Bethany nodded and continued to push through the snow while holding onto poor Julie. She tucked her head down and didn't look up until she bumped into Davy. Davy knelt and nodded forward through a pair of dark trees.

"The house should be right through those trees. And look there..." Davy pointed at what appeared to be a dark silhouette sitting a few feet away. At first, Bethany thought she was seeing a crouching bear. As her gaze focused, the crouching bear turned out to be a parked four-wheeler. "Stay here."

Bethany and Julie watched Davy approach the four-wheeler, bend down, and start messing with something. Maybe the engine or gas tank or battery? They didn't know.

"What did you do?" Bethany asked him when he came back.

"Destroyed the battery connection. That four-wheeler isn't going anywhere," Davy explained. "Now listen, the plan is simple. We scan the house, locate Walley, then you two lure him out into the storm and I put a bullet in his leg or through his shoulder. Our intent is to disable, not to kill. There's been enough killing already."

"Agreed," Bethany and Julie said at the same time.

Davy nodded and moved forward toward the lake house, expecting to see all the lights off. Instead, all the downstairs lights to the house were glowing. He hunkered down behind a tree.

"I wonder why the lights are on?" he asked.

Bethany and Julie joined Davy. Bethany studied the house so dearly loved with uneasy eyes.

"I don't know," she replied.

"I do!" Walley Griffin exploded out from a snow-soaked tree like a hidden ninja. "Get your hands in the air! Now!" he yelled.

All Bethany saw was a man dressed completely in black appear like a shadow seeping out of the fangs of a poisonous snake. She slowly raised her hands and rose to her feet. Julie and Davy followed.

"Drop your rifle!" Walley hollered. Davy reluctantly dropped his rifle. "I got them, Mr. Marizzo! You can come out now!"

Paulie Marizzo stepped out from behind another tree— alone. No hired thugs were with him.

"Very good, Walley," he spoke, hugging a thick coat with frozen arms while tucking his head against a hard wind.

Walley kept a high-powered rifle aimed directly at Bethany. The rifle had a night scope attached to it, which allowed Walley to have clear vision. "I can shoot all of them right now."

"So you betrayed me," Bethany told Mr. Marizzo, her voice calm.

"It's the way the game works, you see," Mr. Marizzo replied. "Learn how to play your pieces. I didn't want to leave too many dead bodies back in town."

"You called Conrad to set me up, didn't you? To make me trust you, right?" Bethany asked, ignoring the icy winds and stinging snow—and frozen feet.

"That's the way of the game." Mr. Marizzo squinted his eyes to see Bethany, Julie, and Davy. "I had a little talk with Mr. Griffin. We worked out a deal. I drove up to the house, and Mr. Griffin agreed to sit and talk with me. He's a nice guy. Real smart. I can use a guy like him."

"That's right," Walley grinned through his ski mask. "Want me to kill them, Mr. Marizzo?"

"It's the way of the game," Mr. Marizzo told Bethany in a tone that ordered Walley to calm down. "After I kill you, your mother will break and tell me where the money is. When I said I didn't want the money, maybe I wasn't being so truthful? Maybe seeing your dead body will loosen your mother's mouth? Maybe I'll give Mr. Griffin a nice reward for helping me."

At first, Bethany struggled to make heads or tails of what was happening. Then something clicked. *Walley Griffin...I guess he's not so stupid after all...and maybe Mr. Marizzo is.*

"Mr. Marizzo, for once in your life, I think you overplayed your cards. Right, Walley?"

A hideous, murderous grin exploded across Walley's face. It was finally time to capture the king.

Before Mr. Marizzo could move, Walley spun around, plugged the old man with a bullet, and turned his rifle back on Bethany without blinking an eye.

"Now, let's talk about that money," he growled as the body of Paulie Marizzo entered a white tomb.

"How about we not?" Bethany replied, spotting movement behind Walley. "I thought you were staying in town?" she called out.

Walley spun around again. As he did, a single bullet erupted through the stormy air and tore into his right hand. Walley let out a loud holler filled with pain, dropped his rifle, and grabbed his right hand with his left hand.

"Don't move! Stay where I can see you!" Riley rushed forward out of the dark woods with a deputy at his side. "Take him down!"

The deputy with Riley tackled Walley down to the ground like a professional linebacker and slapped a pair of handcuffs onto the killer.

Bethany dropped her head. "It's over," she whispered in a voice that sounded shaky rather than relieved. "All the bad guys are dead. Evil kills evil at times."

"My hand! I'll kill you!" Walley screamed in pain, spitting snow out of his mouth. "I'll kill you all!"

"Get him down the mountain...and Donald, good work," Riley told a deputy who was earning his legs. Donald smiled from ear to ear, then dragged Walley off—he wasn't such an inept deputy after all, Riley thought.

He walked over to Bethany, Julie, and Davy on slow legs.

"The phone in Justine's kitchen was bugged. I had to make my act seem real," he told everyone briskly. "The truth of the matter is, once I found out Paulie Marizzo was involved in all of this, I knew Pine Lakes was in real trouble. The only way out was to let—"

"All the bad guys kill each other off?" Bethany asked.

"Sometimes, Ms. Lights, that's the only way." Riley

scanned the three dark, frozen faces. "I have Mr. Marizzo's daughter in custody. The woman isn't a stone wall. She's blabbing her mouth off as we speak. She'll break even more once she finds out that Mr. Marizzo is dead."

Julie stood stunned. "Is this the way justice is handled?" she asked, confused. "I thought cops were supposed to take the bad guys alive?"

"Ms. Walsh, long ago, I crash-landed in a field. I was blamed for the crash even though evidence showed that the transport plane I was flying had mechanical problems. I was thrown out of the navy on a lame medical discharge. After that day, I learned that sometimes to protect yourself and those around you, a man has to step outside the laws created by a system that is corrupt itself. I hope you can understand that." He paused, solemn. "Pine Lakes will be shaken up for a while, but the only people who died were the bad guys and that was my goal: to crash land and make sure every innocent person survived the crash. Pine Lakes is a family community, and I'm a small-town sheriff. Understand?" He nodded toward the lake house. "You two ladies go on to the house and stay there until morning, and that's a direct order. Davy, you're going to have to help me get Mr. Marizzo's body down the mountain."

"Come on, honey." Bethany took Julie's hand, and without saying another word, walked her friend away from dark, snowy woods howling with misery.

They made their way directly into a warm house that sighed with joy when Bethany entered. Bethany quickly ripped off her ski mask and began stomping snow off her boots.

"At least the built-in generators are working. Good. I intend to take an hour-long hot shower."

"Love," Julie struggled to speak as she removed the ski mask covering her lovely face. "Should I try and make sense of any of this?"

"No," Bethany said bluntly. "Julie, honey, we stepped in a wild hornet's nest at the wrong time. I'm sure that in the next hundred years, our minds might understand this mess. But for now, I don't want to think about anything but a hot shower, a hot meal, and a soft bed."

Julie stomped the snow off her boots. "We should be home in the arms of two loving husbands right now, love. Goodness, I left London to seek peace, and now I feel like I'm Nancy Drew's twin." She glanced around the house. "I suppose we should be grateful that we're even alive, and that Sarah found out who called and threatened me. I'll be able to sleep a little easier tonight. Tomorrow, I'll call my son."

Bethany reached out and patted Julie's arm with a loving hand. "Go on upstairs and take a nice, hot shower, honey. I'll make us some coffee and a bite to eat."

"Do you think it's safe? I mean, love, are there any more hidden monsters lurking about?" Julie asked.

"Honey, I think all the monsters are dead. The house is"— Bethany turned and locked the front door—"safe."

Julie let out a tired sigh and nodded. "Yes, I feel that we're safe, too. I'll be upstairs if you need me, love. Hopefully, you won't."

"Only if I burn the coffee."

Bethany saw Julie off and watched her friend crawl up a pair of sleepy stairs on exhausted legs. "Bless her sweet heart. She's a very faithful friend. I'm blessed."

Once Julie was safely upstairs, Bethany walked into a warm, brightly lit kitchen. She dragged her daddy's old gun out of her coat pocket.

"Well, Daddy," she spoke in a tired voice, setting the gun down onto a lonely kitchen table. "I made it through another case. I can't say I had this case in complete control, but I think I did better than last time. I don't think I did so well when I was trapped on Ice Mountain. I could have done worse, I suppose. Life is certainly pushing me in a strange direction. I would love for Snow Falls to have peace, but now I feel like I've entered a strange new world I can't understand."

Bethany scanned the kitchen slowly. A flood of memories rushed into her heart as her eyes moved about. "It'll take time for me to understand what happened here in Pine Falls. I think Sheriff Murphy was smart to keep this entire mess hidden from the public eye. He handled everything in a way that had to be, I guess. I feel like I was simply a pawn in the game."

A hard wind struck the back door. Bethany jumped a little and then relaxed. "Well, the game is over. All I can do is learn from it." She sat down at the kitchen table. "So Daddy, you know I bought the coffee shop you and I visited the time we went to Snow Falls together. I also bought a cabin. I'm happy in Snow Falls. I know Mother isn't happy that I moved so far away, but I needed to be on my own."

Bethany forced the events of the last few days out of her mind and focused on speaking to her daddy. After her discussion, Bethany began cooking a plate of grilled cheese sandwiches and a pot of vegetable beef stew—she even found a cake to bake. By the time Julie entered the kitchen wearing a thick, warm, blue bath robe, Bethany was humming to herself as she wrapped chocolate frosting around the sides of a yellow cake.

"Smells delicious, love." Julie beamed, spotting a warm meal waiting for her on the kitchen table.

"Sit down, honey. We'll eat when I finish the cake." Bethany offered a relaxed smile.

Julie's nose crinkled. "Uh, love, are you okay?"

"I talked to my daddy and realized that the new life I've entered is going to take time to figure out and that I'm not perfect," Bethany explained. She pointed to the back door. "Julie, somewhere out there is a shadow that I'm going to have to face alone. I don't know how I know that, but I do. And right now, I'm feeling as if I'm being taken through a training course of sorts to prepare myself for the fight. I can't explain what I felt while I talked to Daddy...and right now, on this night, it's better if I don't try." She licked a little frosting off her finger and nodded. "Now, let's eat, because tomorrow we're packing up and going back home to Snow Falls—after I call Mother, of course—and find out what the deal is about the money. That part remains a mystery."

Julie simply laughed. "Your mother might not be as innocent as she appears. But right now, who cares, love? Let's eat! That cake looks scrumptious!"

Bethany carried the cake she'd baked over to the kitchen table, sat down before a plate and bowl that held delicious treats, and began talking to Julie about everything except...murder. Bethany figured she had plenty of time to think about the "Pine Lakes Case" in the coming days. For the time being, she hungered for a hot meal and peace of mind.

Far away in Snow Falls, Sarah Spencer walked into a warm kitchen after placing the baby twins down for a good night's rest. She walked over to a closed kitchen door, placed her hand up against it, and closed her eyes.

"Bethany, your fight with the shadows is just beginning. But don't worry, I'll be here for you. You have a difficult, dangerous battle ahead of you."

Outside in the frozen, snowy night, Sarah saw a snowman appear, wearing a leather jacket and eating a candy cane. *Let it snow, Sarah. But for Bethany, this time...oh...let it snow...let it snow...let it snow...*

more from wendy

about wendy meadows

Wendy Meadows is a USA Today bestselling author whose stories showcase women sleuths. To date, she has published dozens of books, which include her popular Sweetfern Harbor series, Sweet Peach Bakery series, and Alaska Cozy series, to name a few. She lives in the "Granite State" with her husband, two sons, two mini pigs and a lovable Labradoodle.

Join Wendy's newsletter to stay up-to-date with new releases. As a subscriber, you'll also get BLACKVINE MANOR, the complete series, for FREE!

Join Wendy's Newsletter Here
wendymeadows.com/cozy